THAT WAS ONLY THE REHEARSAL

CAROLINE LOUISE

1

June 13, 2019

It was 9:06 when I first heard the sirens wailing. Like most people, I had snuggled up under my covers, clad in bunny pajamas, getting ready to pretend to be asleep for the next few hours. My hand clutched my phone as I began the grueling task of deciding what to watch on YouTube. "Haley! Downstairs!" my mother's commanding voice called from, obviously, downstairs.

"Coming!" I shrieked in response. I was annoyed that she had roused me from my bed just as I was beginning to get comfortable. *If what she needs to tell me is so important,* I thought, *then why doesn't she just come to me?* Nevertheless, I tied up my hair as I bounced down the steps.

Cops. Everywhere. Cops sitting around the wooden table where my mom, dad, and I cracked jokes nearly every morning at breakfast. The counter, the fridge, everywhere: covered in unwelcome men with squawking walkie-talkies. I hated that they had already seemed to infiltrate my life. Being treated like a stranger in my own house was bad, but even worse was the look on my mother's face. Usually, my mother was full of life. Faith Hansen had an easy happiness that seemed to spread to anyone in her proximity. Her playful blonde bob matched her sparkling blue eyes. I loved how much I looked like her, how similar people thought we were. But she looked different now. New lines that I had never noticed before marked her face; her already pale complexion had turned ghostly white. "What are they doing here?" I questioned. My voice cracked with anxiety.

"Honey, I think you need to sit down for this," my mother replied as tears started to brim around her thick eyelashes. Complying with her request, I lowered myself into the chair in the corner next to the cabinet. If I wasn't already, I was starting to worry now. "The police—" my mother started before sobs began to rack her thin frame.

A nearby officer put his hand on my mother's shoulder and started where she had left off. He was tall and clean-shaven and, despite his professional air, seemed remorseful. "We have taken your father into custody," he said.

"For what?" I stammered. "I—I don't understand." The officer's eyes turned to the ground. All was silent for a few moments until I mustered the strength to speak again. Gathering all the energy I had left, I acknowledged the elephant in the room. "Why?" I asked. It was a simple question with a simple answer that turned out to be not so simple.

The officer raised his head and brought his sad eyes to mine. "For the murder of Hannah Schulz."

. . .

Okay, you're probably thinking: *Who the heck is Hannah Schulz?* Why did my father, Dan Hansen, kill her? She was ordinary, with medium-length, glossy brown hair and a myriad of freckles that wouldn't make you look twice, but she was so much more than ordinary to me. We'd grown up together and we were thick as thieves, as close as sisters. She wasn't the easiest to love, I'll admit. Hannah was the type of person who would tell you the truth no matter how much it hurt because she knew it was what you needed to hear—even when you didn't want to. But Hannah always knew the right thing to do: how to make you feel better, and how to make you laugh, smile, and cry.

I can tell you how he did it, but the *why* is a bit more blurry. I won't get into the details because frankly, I don't want to remember it, let alone talk about it. But I think it's important to tell you that on that fateful night, Dan Hansen wrote *For Haley* in Hannah's blood.

After June 13th, nobody in the town of Wilake would look at me or my mother the same way. I wasn't just Haley Hansen anymore. I was Haley Hansen, daughter of Dan Hansen, murderer. It was like I had permanently been stained by my own blood, and you can't change blood.

Some people, namely Hannah's parents, couldn't look at us at all. Their scorn was the most painful of all to me. I wanted Hannah's mother to hug me and tell me it was all right, and for Hannah's father to tell me it wasn't my fault. But they didn't, because they couldn't. Perhaps it was my fault.

That was why we moved to Fort Vepar: to escape the watchful eyes of judgment. We sold the house and my mother packed her things—furniture, dishes, bits and pieces that reminded her of a good life. Me? I only packed a duffel bag full of clothes and a picture of Hannah.

I didn't want to remember Wilake at all. I wanted to wake up a new human being with no past, nothing but a here and now. But that's not really how life works. I could try to be new, but the old me was still there, full of nightmares and memories. When people in Fort Vepar ask me about my father, I say he's out of the picture.

But he's not and never will be.

2

November 8, 2019

The speaker above me let out an electronic squeal, jarring me awake. I looked around the classroom to see if anyone had noticed me doze off. They hadn't. All attention was turned to the rusty box on the wall rather than our elderly English teacher, much to his dismay.

Eventually it spoke, but not before making some rather obnoxious clangs and screeches. "All students are to report to the auditorium for a mandatory assembly in ten minutes."

With a beep, it stopped.

That's weird, I thought. We rarely had assemblies or gathered in the auditorium. But no matter. We were happy enough to get an excuse to leave English class. Before our teacher could protest, we were out the door and making our way to the auditorium.

While everyone else paired up or walked to the auditorium in groups, I walked alone. I hadn't made an effort to get to know my new classmates that well. I only really had one friend and a few acquaintances who only knew my first name. I doubt that half of the class had noticed that I had transferred this year.

But that was A-okay because I had Noah. He was pretty much the only thing keeping me sane since we had moved to Fort Vepar. While my other classmates ignored me, he had actively made an effort to get to know me.

I was hesitant at first—scared to make new friends. Some part of me felt like it would be a betrayal of Hannah's memory. Nevertheless, I succumbed to his charm. "Haley!" I heard from behind me. *Speak of the devil.*

Noah broke into a slow jog to catch up with me; he was followed by his friend Jonas.

It wasn't a surprise that Noah had other friends, and it was actually quite surprising that he didn't have more. He could make anyone smile, and he could crack jokes without a moment's hesitation. Noah always seemed to know the right thing to say and when to say it.

He was tall and attractive, but not the kind of attractive that made a big deal about itself. He was tanned, with bright brown eyes and dark hair that fell just above his chin. Jonas wasn't too different from Noah, except his complexion was as pale as snow, kind of like a pale shadow of Noah. Despite the similarities, we weren't that close.

Naturally, as the shadow, he was the more soft-spoken of the two. He was quiet where Noah was loud, seemingly feeling perfectly comfortable with fading into the background. Perhaps this was why we had only talked a handful of times. He didn't seem all that interested in me. It was either that or Jonas hated people, but Noah brought out the best in him, as he did with everyone.

Our trio made the trek through the dimly lit hallway up to the auditorium. In a lot of ways, Fort Vepar High School wasn't too different from my old one. The same navy metal lockers lined the halls surrounding the tan linoleum floors, lit by square overhead lights. All in all, it conformed with a very popular look in America's schools. *A dimly lit path to a brighter future ...*

Noah was the first to break the silence. "What do you think the assembly's about?"

"Probably your blatant disregard for the dress code," I teased. Noah snorted. Our principal, Mrs. Donahue, had been trying to get Noah lifetime detention since the beginning of the year for chronically violating the dress code. But his sweatpants and hoodies were always just clean enough and not quite saggy enough to cross the line, and since his teachers loved him, no one was going out of their way to ding him for a violation.

"Okay, but like, seriously," Noah reiterated.

I shrugged.

"Beats me," said Jonas, although he seemed uneasy.

"Whatever it is can't be that bad," I said. "The only slightly scandalous thing that's happened since I got here is when Suzie Morgan snuck her ferret into school for two hours."

"So you're proposing that this is a threat-level ferret assembly?" joked Noah.

"Maybe two." He snickered as we entered the auditorium, another shoutout to American high school architecture.

Calling it an auditorium was a bit generous. In reality, it was what used to be the gym before the school was remodeled. It had tall brick walls and a laminated wooden floor, basketball court lines included. At one end of the room was a stage with a microphone in the center, and the rest of the room was filled with fold-out chairs.

Right away, it was easy to tell that this assembly was about something more serious than a ferret (or two). A few teachers stood on the stage and chattered among themselves nervously, occasionally stealing glances at the students. Mrs. Donahue looked the most nervous of them all. Her eyes appeared more sunken and her lips tighter than usual.

The teachers' anxiety had already caused some tension among the students. They too had started to hypothesize the meaning of our gathering. I couldn't make out any full sentences, but I could hear a few snippets of their conversations. The general gist of it was *vandalism, anti-drugs assembly, that one kid who vapes in the bathroom getting expelled …*

The only ones that seemed completely unaffected by the drama were the group that Noah sometimes jokingly called "the Heathers," like the group of popular girls in the musical. Of course, they weren't really "Heathers," they were Rebecca Martinez, Sarah Rhodes, and Allison Vos.

Rebecca was a lot quieter and less athletic than the other two girls, which apparently made her less desirable. I didn't understand why, though. She could definitely be a model, with brown skin and dark brown hair that complemented each other perfectly. I'd always liked her. I thought that we could be friends if either of us was willing to branch out a bit more.

Then there was Sarah. I had nothing personal against her, I just hated her. She was utterly unoriginal and full of herself. Just like Rebecca, she could have been a model. Sarah had glossy black hair that fell halfway down her back, light olive skin, and brown eyes. She tried to copy Allison's every mannerism, from the way she talked to the way she dressed.

I shouldn't be so critical, I thought. Who am I to judge? My life is a hot mess.

That left Allison. She was built like a Barbie doll: tall and slim, with blue eyes and blonde hair. Despite her good looks, her personality was her standout feature. She was popular but not condescending, adored but not idolized. That was what I admired about her—how she could be so aware of who she was but not use it against others.

What was surprising to me was that Allison wasn't among their ranks today. Without her there, Rebecca and Sarah seemed almost bored with each other, like Allison was the spark making them animated.

It reminded me of Noah, Jonas, and me. Without Noah, we would never have been friends, but if I had to choose a seat in class, it might as well be next to Jonas.

After five or so minutes of standing around, we eventually settled in our seats. Mrs. Donahue made her way to the microphone in the center of the stage, although her usual confident saunter was noticeably missing. She tapped the microphone a few times, sending an electronic thump through the crowd. She cleared her throat. "I'm sure it has come to your attention that we are not gathered here today in regular circumstances," she began. "An hour ago, we received the very difficult news that—" Mrs. Donahue's voice cracked with emotion and a wave of uncertainty. Nevertheless, she composed herself and continued. "We have received the very difficult news that junior Allison Vos has passed away unexpectedly this morning."

A few muffled cries broke out, but most people were stunned out of any reaction. Mrs. Donahue put her speech on pause to let the initial shock sink in. Whether you knew Allison personally or not, you knew her. None of us had ever imagined this happening.

I can't breathe.

"As a community, we are saddened by this tragedy," she said. "We will do everything in our power to accommodate any emotions you may be feeling right now. The counseling department will be open to students at all hours. We are also working on setting up a helpline in case anyone needs it."

If Mrs. Donahue was still talking, I didn't hear it. The noise around me was completely drowned out.

It can't be true.

Poor Rebecca was starting to whimper. Tears plastered her dark hair to her cheeks, blending with running mascara. Sarah walked her out of the room, emotionless—which struck me as odd.

It was Sarah who had seemed closer to Allison. Rebecca had always seemed more like the third wheel in their friendship. But as I had learned, appearances can be deceiving.

Yet *she seemed so healthy ...*

Once Rebecca had been escorted out of the auditorium, Mrs. Donahue continued to address us. "We would like to hold a memorial service for Allison this upcoming Sunday to celebrate her life." She looked up. "I understand that it may be difficult to process all of this, so I am giving you the rest of the day off. Check your email these next few days for any important updates."

Then it hit me. *How did she die?*

3

In the midst of the silence, I got up and bolted out of the auditorium. I could feel hundreds of eyes on me, but I didn't care—I couldn't think. I just wanted to get away.

No, no, no, no, no. What a fool I was making out of myself; I barely knew her. *I can't breathe.* Everything was becoming cold again like the night Hannah died. Something seemed off about Allison dying. *She was in peak health and seemed perfectly happy,* I thought. I needed to clear my head. School was out for the day anyways. I ran and ran until I reached the forest-green doors between the school and the outside world, but I didn't stop there. My final destination was over the chain-link fence protecting the woods from the school, a popular destination for me when I wanted to avoid going home ... which was often, nowadays. If you walked thirty or so feet away from the fence, you would find a shallow stream flowing underneath a canopy of trees. One tree lay lifeless on the bank of the stream, providing seating for anyone who dared venture into the woods. But that wasn't the best part about it. An impossibly large rock looked down on all of this. It stood about six feet off the ground. I promptly climbed it. It was covered in pretty vulgar graffiti.

That was what stood out to me. There were probably hundreds of places that looked exactly like this around the world, but the graffiti claimed that this was mine. But maybe not only mine. Noah and Jonas came bounding through the trees, interrupting my much-needed peace and quiet. "Haley, are you okay?" asked Noah.

"Yeah, fine. I guess," I replied.

"I don't know, you seemed pretty upset back there. Is there something you need to talk about?"

Hannah, I thought. *I need to talk about Hannah.* But instead, I just shook my head *no*. This didn't seem to satisfy Noah. He frowned and looked intently at me, as if he was trying to break down a door and walk into my mind. Jonas, for his part, just stared at me with a sad look. I knew that had our roles been reversed, I would have felt the same need to understand. But I couldn't help thinking that if they knew about Hannah, they would have second thoughts about our friendship. Though truth be told, I'm not sure Jonas thought of us as friends at all.

The two boys began climbing the Rock to join me, but Noah suddenly stopped. His face went blank. "I completely forgot!" He frowned. "I promised Rebecca that I'd help her study for physics."

Jonas groaned. "Do you think physics is Rebecca's biggest concern right now?" He was right. We had all seen Rebecca's breakdown in assembly. She was clearly in no shape to be studying at the moment. I don't think anyone in our school was.

"I don't know, man. She texted to tell me that she still wanted to study."

I perked up. "Isn't that kind of weird, though?" I said. "Like, didn't she just lose one of her closest friends?"

Noah shrugged. "Yeah, but everyone grieves in their own way, I guess." True. I couldn't blame her. After Hannah was killed, I was a mess. I couldn't think straight. I could barely remember who I was or even accept that Hannah was gone. But after a while I just became numb. I lost two people that day: Hannah and the man I thought my father was.

Noah waved goodbye and started jogging through the bushes back toward the school, leaving Jonas and me alone on the rock. Jonas turned to me and asked, "Do you want me to walk you home?" This was a bit unusual, since he had never struck me as particularly chivalrous or sociable. But I was somewhat intrigued by his suggestion.

"Sure," I said, and jumped off the rock. We began to hike through fallen tree branches and climbed over the fence that led us to the sidewalk. My house wasn't too far from the school. As a matter of fact, nothing was too far away from the school. Fort Vepar was small enough that you could travel everywhere by bike or even on foot. That scared me sometimes. I would lie awake at night fearing that someone in this little town would find out about my father and we'd have to leave Fort Vepar just like we'd left Wilake.

After an awkward silence, we started walking down the sidewalk. Jonas turned to me. "Don't you think it's weird that we barely know each other?"

That took me by surprise. "What do you mean?"

"Like, we're always hanging out together with Noah, but we barely talk. I feel like I hardly know who you are."

Ouch. "A lot of people don't," I said, then immediately thought, *Why'd I say that?*

He glanced over at me. "That doesn't mean they don't want to. Trust me, you could have a lot more friends if you just tried talking to people."

I shrugged. I had never really considered getting to know anyone in Fort Vepar. For me, it was just the place we were staying right now before we got chased out by rumors. It wasn't permanent, not like I'd thought Wilake was. "Okay."

"Okay what?"

"Let's get to know each other better," I said. "You said it yourself, it's a bit weird that I don't know the slightest thing about you." Jonas laughed. "What's so funny?"

"Nothing. I just didn't see this coming. I thought you'd roll your eyes at me."

"Wow, you think highly of me."

He winced and shrugged his shoulders. "Sorry. That's not what I meant."

"I was just kidding." I laughed. "Okay, okay. Twenty questions."

"Twenty questions? Geez, I think the last time I played that game was in sixth grade." I punched him in the arm jokingly. "Ouch! Fine."

"All right: question one," I said. "What's your biggest pet peeve?"

Jonas smirked. "Slow walkers. Maybe mysterious girls named Haley Hansen punching me out of nowhere? But probably slow walkers."

I laughed. "It wasn't a punch, it was a light tap."

"Sure, sure," said Jonas. "Moving on. What's your biggest pet peeve?"

I bit my lip in concentration. What was my biggest pet peeve? I guess it could be people chewing with their mouths open or paying for shipping, but those didn't seem right. What understanding would Jonas gain about me from my hatred of paying for shipping? Finally, I decided. "People misjudging me."

He turned to look me in the eyes. "How do you think people misjudge you?"

"I'm not sure." I paused. "It's like what you said about people wanting to be friends with me. Like, they just assume that they know what type of person I am."

He smirked. "And what type of person are you?"

I turned around and started walking backward. By now we had reached the part of town with the unkempt grass, the area where I lived. This was my signal to let Jonas go. "I guess you'll have to find out."

4

Home not-so-sweet home. You could hardly call the Hansen house welcoming. It was light green, which on a bad day reminded me strongly of vomit. Overgrown weeds lined the path to the front door, which was wooden and had paint chipping off the bottom.

The curtains were closely drawn. Like many of the houses on the block, it was small, with an aging white picket fence, a tribute to when the house might have been more favorable. All in all, it was not a place you'd smile walking past.

But the inside was basically soul-deflating—not only the décor but the mood. Right now, I knew my mother would be peering through the curtains looking for that someone—or someones—who she was sure was always watching us. Coming home from school was always a fat reality check.

At this point, she was only a shell of my real mother. She was vaguely similar in appearance, but her opposite in personality. The mother I used to have was full of life, always the first to offer to chaperone a field trip or pitch in at a bake sale. Now she could barely leave the house to get groceries, and when she did, she needed a day or two to recover afterward.

I unlocked the front door and it creaked open. My mother was leaning against the doorframe, arms crossed, bug-eyed at the sight of another human being. She looked like someone who had just stumbled out of a bunker after five years without any human contact.

"I heard about that girl at school, the dead one. They sent out an email this afternoon."

I rolled my eyes. "I'm surprised you even open your email anymore." I stormed off to my room, which was difficult, considering it was only a few feet away. Storming off usually requires a longer path of escape, but I was a pro by now. We lived in a small house, where I couldn't really escape my mother if I tried.

"Haley!" she yelled as I slammed the door.

I put in my earbuds and closed my eyes. Music flooded my ears as I tried to drown out my thoughts. She had no right to be mad at me. In the past few months, my mother had all but abandoned me in every respect. When my dad went to prison, we lost our primary source of income. My mother blew all the family's savings on trying to find my dad the best lawyers, but she knew it was pointless, since we all knew he'd done it. If you'd asked him, he'd have been the first to tell you that.

Despite his unique honesty, it still took her about two months to fully process and accept that her husband was a killer. After the verdict, we sold the house and used the profit to move here. She refused to get a job, claiming she wasn't ready. But it had been more than six months now and she still wasn't ready, and she never would be, from the look of things.

I gazed out the window. The sky had become enshrouded with clouds. Soon, they began pelting rain down on Fort Vepar. That was when my tears started coming, running like a river down my cheeks. *Other people have it worse,* I told myself. Sometimes I needed a reminder to get over myself. I sniffled and dried my tears with the sleeve of my sweatshirt.

My phone buzzed and I grunted as I tried to reach it. I wasn't in the mood, but it was from Jonas. There was no point wallowing in my self-pity anyway.

Jonas: question 2. do you believe in ghosts?

Haley: Capitalization?

irrelevant

I'm not a die-hard believer, but I wouldn't be that surprised if they're real.

elaborate.

I don't think that foggy white things follow us around everywhere, but I think other things can be ghosts.

i get that. my mom has this creepy ceramic duck that i'm 50% sure is haunted.

Alright, your turn. Do you believe in ghosts?

heck yeah.

Elaborate.

ha ha. i just think that it's kinda comforting.

Are you seriously telling me that you think the idea of dead people walking around your house is comforting?

no! i just think of the memories, you know? like, they never really leave you i guess. maybe that's why people see ghosts, as a message that something is unresolved or whatever.

I typed *I know what you mean* and turned off my phone. I knew exactly what he meant. Too many ghosts haunted the Hansen house.

My eyes grew heavy. I hadn't noticed how tired I was until this moment. I allowed myself to close my eyes for a moment, which then became two hours. My phone buzzed again from my nightstand. Initially, I just ignored it. I thought it was probably a group chat or something, but then it began to ring violently. I thrashed my half-asleep arm across the bed and over the nightstand to retrieve the device.

Eleven missed calls, all from Noah. My fingers slowly drifted to my mouth. Old habits die hard, I guess. I always bit my fingernails when I was nervous, and this time I had a good cause. Noah wasn't the type to be so anxious—he was usually laid back, and always took things in his stride. I entered my passcode and dialed him. The phone didn't even beep once before he picked up.

"Haley! Where are you? Why haven't you been returning my calls?"

"Calm down. I was taking a nap." He sighed audibly on the other end of the phone. "What's up?"

"It's about Allison." *Allison?*

"What do you mean?" I asked. "Did they reschedule the memorial or something?" Of course they hadn't rescheduled the memorial. Whatever had happened, it was worth eleven missed calls.

"It's all over Snapchat." Of course, everything seemed to be on Snapchat these days, but I hadn't felt obligated to make an account. From what I could tell, it was basically a vapid wasteland.

"What is?"

"People are saying she was murdered."

"What do you mean?" I asked him, but I knew exactly what he meant. He couldn't have been more clear. Yet somehow my brain couldn't fully grasp what he was saying. *Allison. Was. Murdered.*

"You know how I was tutoring Rebecca after school today, right?" I nodded, then quickly remembered that Noah couldn't see me and said yes.

"So we were studying in the science room, and then Mrs. Donahue came in to get Rebecca."

"Why?"

"To question her or something. They took in Sarah and Steven too." Steven was Allison's boyfriend. He was handsome with broad shoulders, dark brown eyes, and long black hair that all came together. I didn't have anything against Steven, but I had always thought he was a little big-headed.

I gasped. "Do they think one of them did it?"

I could hear Noah shudder over the phone. It was scary to think that one of our classmates could be a murderer. "I don't think so. I texted Rebecca to make sure she was okay, and she said that they just wanted to know where Allison was last night and when was the last time she heard from her, so I think she might be in the clear."

I sighed in relief. I couldn't imagine Rebecca even swatting a fly, much less murdering someone. But Steven and Sarah? Not so long ago I would have told you *Of course not. People in small towns don't go around murdering kids.* But things had changed.

Now I knew differently, so I started to think of murder through a lens of reality. Sarah was obviously jealous of Allison. Could she have killed her to replace her? And Steven? Maybe he just got tired of her.

As sick as those thoughts were, they had to be considered. But Sarah and Steven didn't seem like murderers, if that instinct of mine even made sense anymore.

"Wow," I said. "This is a lot to process." We were both quiet for a minute. Neither of us was quite sure what to say. "Well, see you at the memorial on Sunday?"

"Yeah."

"Okay. Bye."

"Wait, Haley."

"Yeah?"

"Stay safe." He hung up.

5

Early Sunday morning, I lay awake thinking about Allison.

Sometimes Allison had reminded me of Hannah; they shared the same cheery personality and infectious smile. Maybe that was why I was afraid to get close to her; every time I saw her, it brought back the terrible ache of losing Hannah.

I picked up my phone: 2 a.m. No point trying to sleep now. I rubbed my eyes, peeled back my covers, and walked over to the closet. My closet was fairly small. A few sweatshirts and pairs of leggings hung on hangers attached to the bottom of a shelf. The rest of the closet was mostly filled with untouched moving boxes full of junk my mother had brought over from the old house. Half a year in, and there had been no talk of moving. It was as good a time as any to start unpacking (or throwing away) everything.

I grunted as I heaved one of the heavier boxes onto the carpet. With a sigh, I sat on the floor and started unpacking old family photos, porcelain elephants, and other oddities. Over half of the stuff went straight into my trash bag. *One down, a million to go.*

I began on my second box. This one was almost full to the brim with books and a bunch of journals my mom and dad had written in. I had no idea that my mom had kept them after the move. She probably didn't do it on purpose, just threw everything into the boxes when we were making our jailbreak out of Wilake, running as fast as we possibly could.

I spread the journals across the floor—fifteen in total. I began with one of my mother's. She probably wouldn't care too much if I took a peek. It dated back to almost two years ago. *"December 2nd, 2018. Today I went shopping for Christmas presents for Dan and Haley. They'll be so surprised that I got a new family computer! It was on sale and I'm trying to stay on budget, so a few lucky Hansens are getting extra socks this year. Maybe something for Hannah too. She's been so—"*

I stopped reading. I'd always wondered what my mom did all day when we were gone. I had hoped that it was a little more interesting than this, but I took that thought back. I kind of missed the mundane. Maybe this wasn't boring, just stable. I could use that now.

I threw the journal onto my bed and tossed the rest back into the cardboard box, where they would be shoved back into the depths of my closet. I figured I should try to get some sleep. The day ahead would surely be filled with speeches and tears. That was enough for someone to deal with when they had had eight hours of sleep. I checked my phone to see if anyone was online. Jonas. Even though we weren't the best of friends, I knew the guy was practically a vampire.

I smirked. I hadn't heard from him for a day. Time for another question.

Question 3: What are you doing up so late?

i could ask you the same thing.

Capitalization?

no

Me? Couldn't sleep thinking about the memorial. You?

idk if i'm even going.

I scrunched up my face. What did he mean, he wasn't going? It was the decent thing to do and practically mandatory.

Why not?

is that question 4 i hear? facetime me.

I hesitated. *FaceTime him? What does he want to talk about over FaceTime that he can't over text?* I had to admit, I was intrigued. There was something mysterious about Jonas that I couldn't quite put my finger on. *If I get closer to him,* I thought, *maybe I could find out.* I dialed the number and waited for the chime. Jonas appeared on my screen. His dark hair fell into his eyes, which looked very tired. Even his skin looked paler, and that was saying something. "Are you okay?" I asked. Something about him seemed off.

Jonas rubbed his eyes. "Yeah, just a little tired."

"Do you ever sleep?" I joked.

"Not really," he replied with no hint of emotion. "Too much to think about."

I reclined against my pillow. "I know how that is. What did you want to FaceTime about?"

Jonas sighed, shifting uncomfortably. "You know what? It's nothing. I'll see you tomorrow at the memorial," he said, then hung up.

What just happened? Did Jonas really ask to FaceTime me only to hang up a moment later? I let out a silent but frustrated scream and slammed my phone down on my desk—which unfortunately was followed by my mother howling "Haley!" from the other side of the wall.

I sighed. *Great.* Not only did Jonas hang up on me, now I was going to have to talk to my mother at two in the morning.

She burst into the room, wearing the same clothes she had been wearing all yesterday. And maybe the day before. I suddenly wondered how often she showered nowadays. *Is that a normal thing for someone to be worried about?*

Her graying blonde hair was tousled at all different angles and she clung to her sweater. "For God's sake, Haley, what are you doing awake?"

I frowned. "What are you doing up?" Before I could stop myself, I added, "Is this why you sleep all day and can't look for a job?"

The two of us stared at each other, speechless, my mother's mouth agape as well as mine. Finally, she pursed her lips. "That's not fair."

Heat began to rise to my face. I stood up, getting closer and closer to my mother. "Yeah? Well, you know what else isn't fair? Having to watch you sit around all day and do nothing! I don't even know who you are anymore!"

I paused to catch a breath and slowly started to inch closer to my mom, who was just standing there, blank, weak, and beaten. I suddenly saw fear creep into her eyes, and in a flash I knew exactly what she was thinking. I was just like him.

She began to stumble towards the door.

"You say that you're not ready, but neither was I! I didn't ask Dad to kill my best friend and leave me with a deadbeat for a parent."

She backed out of my room, stumbling into the doorframe as she slid into the hallway. I jumped forward and slammed the door in her face.

As soon as it was closed, my hands flew to my mouth. *What have I done?* Tears started coming hot and fast. I had cried every day for, what? The past three days? That hadn't happened since I'd got here. I sobbed into my arms. I wanted to leave so badly— leave all of this. It didn't matter where I went as long as no one followed me. I could change my name and start over, but that couldn't change my past. Like a freight train in the night surging towards me, I couldn't escape it.

I wiped my tears. After a few minutes, I could no longer hear my mother breathing jaggedly outside my door. I closed my eyes and sighed with relief. I eventually made my way back to the bed and sank into the covers. I must have fallen asleep the moment my head hit the pillow.

6

People always told me that I was just like my father. At the time, I took it as a compliment. We shared the same blue eyes and dimple on our left cheek, although my hair was lighter and wispier than his, closer to my mother's. Our similarities weren't just skin-deep. We both chewed our nails, which angered my mother immensely, and took our coffee iced, with two sugars.

I used to think that we had the same personality too, and shared the same values. My father was a down-to-earth guy, but that didn't mean he wasn't fun. He had a dry sense of humor that I loved and people often told me I had. He valued honesty and family above all else. He was passionate about many things he believed in, which sometimes meant he showed a temper. My dad used to laugh when I got angry and tell me I was fiery just like him. When I came crying to him about a problem, he would always be honest with me, never sugarcoating anything. I sometimes resented it when I was younger, but even then, I knew it was for the best.

But when I'd talk to him about Hannah, he was different. My dad became sullen all of a sudden, silent. When I once told him that Hannah and I had gotten into a big blowout fight, he told me it was all her fault, telling me I should back away from our friendship. Which, though I didn't think much of it at the time, was really odd for all the reasons I mentioned. He was usually even-handed about those kinds of things, saying stuff like *It takes two people to tango and two people to argue*—it wasn't one person making everything happen.

But she apologized profusely the next day, tears and everything. That was a month before my dad murdered her.

Truth be told, Hannah and I argued a lot. But we always made up, because we both knew an argument was like a rain shower—it happened and then the sun would shine again. Nothing we said could break our friendship because we truly loved each other like sisters. I think my dad just snapped and never snapped back. He still thinks he did the right thing, that he violated no moral code whatsoever. He made sure to tell the press that. They may never have leaked my name, but they did write about what happened. Everyone knew about a guy named Dan Hansen who had murdered his daughter's best friend for her. He said she was fake, that she was bad for me, and that she would leave me for other friends. Some sick, sick people still think he's a hero for killing Hannah, but she made mistakes just like any teenage girl.

I don't.

7

Sunday morning, I met Jonas and Noah outside school for the memorial. I was dressed in a formal long black coat that covered my T-shirt and jeans, completed with high black boots. Jonas looked sad. Noah looked tense, but then again, everyone besides Jonas did. Many of my classmates were having a hard time coping with Allison's death, and the fact that people were saying it was murder made it ten times worse. Looking at the sea of students clad in black, I could tell we all had one thing in common: We were scared. We were scared of a potential killer on the loose. Heck, they could be here right now.

I glanced behind me to see a sobbing Rebecca being comforted by a bored Sarah. Out of everyone, Rebecca was having the hardest time coping with Allison's death. Or at least, it appeared that way. I turned to Noah. "Do you think she'll be all right?"

He grimaced. "Yeah, just give her time."

I stole another glance at Rebecca. When the sobbing subsided, tears still streamed down her face as she clung to Sarah. "I didn't know that they were that close," I said.

"Neither did I, but you never know," Noah said, looking me in the eye, but I looked down at my boots.

Jonas looked a little better than he had last night; some color had returned to his face. He said in a low voice, "Do they have any idea who did it?"

Noah's eyes doubled in size, flabbergasted. "Shhh, man. You can't go around saying things like that," he hissed quietly at Jonas.

"I'm just saying. They won't tell us anything. It's frustrating," Jonas said. "If they just told us what happened, then maybe everyone wouldn't be standing around looking for a murderer. The cops have some idea who killed her."

"Jonas!" Noah hissed again.

"Just saying."

Mrs. Donahue emerged from the school and opened the doors, then placed a sign with directions out front. She ushered the people that had already gathered into the auditorium. A fold-out plastic table hugged the wall, covered in a Costco cracker spread and juice boxes. *Classy*, I thought. The walls were covered in pictures of Allison taken by her friends and family. The Voses stood near the center of the auditorium around a circle of chairs, whispering among themselves.

Melanie Vos, Allison's sister who was two grades below us, sent me a look from across the room. She didn't just look upset but enraged. At me? I tilted my head at her in response. Melanie rolled her eyes and looked away. Weird. I knew she was Allison's sister, but I had never talked to her. Did she even know who I really was? No one did. And I hadn't even been friends with Allison.

Maybe she was planning to shoot everyone a look. Melanie was going to have some tough days ahead and was full of anger. I knew how that felt. After Hannah died, I stayed mad at everyone and everything.

I grabbed a lemonade from the snack spread and rejoined Noah and Jonas just as Mrs. Vos and Mrs. Donahue walked onto the stage.

Mrs. Donahue clapped her hands and spoke into a microphone. "If I may have your attention, please? The memorial honoring the life of Allison Vos is about to begin. Please be seated in the circle of chairs in front." She handed the microphone to Allison's mom. Once everyone was seated, Mrs. Vos began to speak.

"First of all, I'd like to welcome everyone who was able to join us here today." Her face grew red as tears gushed from her eyes. "Thank you for joining us today to celebrate Allison's life.

Please stand." She cleared her throat. "'Truly, truly I say to you, whoever hears my word and believes Him who sent me has eternal life. He does not come to judgment, but has passed from life to death.' John 5:24." She took a step back and there was a moment of silence.

All eyes were on Rebecca as she began to cry again. After a minute or so, Mrs. Vos spoke again. "I would like to invite some of Allison's friends to say a few words. Feel free to share a favorite memory or story of Allison if you would like."

Sarah stood first. Without so much as a trembling hand, she removed a slip of paper from the pocket of her faux fur coat and gave a sad smile in the direction of Allison's family. "Allison was my best friend, and I miss her every day."

Mrs. Vos put her hand on her heart and started to nod, with the stoic Mr. Vos's hand on her shoulder.

Sarah looked down at her piece of paper again. "Allison will be remembered for how kind she was to everyone around her and how much she loved her family."

I had expected her to say more, but she sat down.

Rebecca exhaled loudly and left the room. "She pulled a Haley," I heard someone snicker quietly. Sarah turned around, looking to see where Rebecca had disappeared to, then got up and followed her out.

Sarah's little speech, if you could even call it that, had deflated me. All Sarah could say about her death was two generic sentences she'd probably googled. *That's the best you can do for your best friend?* I would have poured my heart out about Hannah, given the chance. But of course, I wasn't invited to her memorial or funeral. All my thoughts and prayers were silent.

Mrs. Vos glanced sideways to see Rebecca and Sarah's exit, but it didn't seem to bother her. "Would anyone else like to share a story?" she asked.

I looked around the circle. Most people were holding back tears, others looked bored, and some were looking at their feet, not sure what they were feeling.

I couldn't take it. *Do any of these people even care about Allison, or are they just pretending to so they won't look heartless?* I stood up. "May I speak?"

Mrs. Vos looked at me with a dazed expression on her face. "Um, yes, of course, dear."

I began. "If I'm being honest, I wasn't very close to Allison." Jonas stretched his back in the chair, now engaged. If people hadn't been paying attention before, they certainly were now. "But what I could tell was that she was a special person. Not once did I hear her talk down to anybody or make anyone feel left out. Whether you knew her personally or not, she brightened your day at least once."

I sat down. "Thank you," mouthed Mrs. Vos. Large, heavy tears continued to pour from her eyes.

For a while we sat in silence, then more people began sharing stories about Allison. Some were as simple as the time she lent them a pencil. After a few minutes, I felt my bladder tickle and I excused myself to use the restroom. I walked out of the auditorium and past my science classroom to get to the bathroom. *Was it just three days ago that Allison was here too without a care in the world?* I shook my head. It was better not to think about it. People might sometimes expect the worst, but they're always surprised when it actually happens.

The school's bathroom was oddly constructed, shaped like an L and connected to the locker room by a heavy door. Just as I was about to flush the toilet, I heard muffled shouts coming from around the corner, behind the locker room door. *Didn't anyone notice me come in here?* I silently flipped back the lock on my stall and tiptoed to the locker room door and pressed my ear against it. Two familiar female voices were engaged in a shouting match.

"Stop acting so darn fake!" *Rebecca?* Rebecca.

"It's not my fault that I don't have a meltdown every time someone talks about her!" And Sarah. I should have guessed.

"Maybe if you cared about her enough you would."

They went silent for a beat. I imagined Rebecca glaring at Sarah. "All I'm saying is she was your best friend. Show some respect," said Rebecca, dialing down the volume a bit.

"Yeah, but she wasn't yours. Just because you're suddenly obsessed with her doesn't mean I didn't care about her. Grow up."

I gasped. Footsteps, presumably Sarah's, were approaching the door. I tiptoed into a stall and put my feet on the toilet. As Sarah's footsteps got closer, I made the executive decision to stop breathing. I was so concentrated on that, that I lost my balance and almost slipped off the toilet seat, making an obnoxious (and loud) squeaking noise. As I slid, I caught myself on the plastic wall of the toilet stall.

Sarah stopped in her tracks. "Hello?" she called. "Anyone in here?"

I held my breath and closed my eyes, praying for her to go away. Sarah's footsteps got quieter as she prowled back and forth, checking for feet under the stalls. When she didn't find any, she started crawling on the floor. *Wow,* I thought. *She doesn't know when to quit.* It was only a matter of time before she reached mine.

I popped my head under the door just as she was about to reach me. "Fancy seeing you here!" I said, flashing her the biggest smile I could muster.

"Geez, don't be such a creep," Sarah hissed angrily.

"Sorry, I just had to use the bathroom. It's not my fault you're looking under all the stalls." I stepped backward and flushed the toilet to make myself more convincing. When she didn't ease her scowl, I put my hands up. "I come in peace," I told her. As I tried to walk toward the sink to wash my hands, Sarah grabbed my shoulder and spun me around. She looked thoroughly unamused.

"How much did you hear?"

I feigned confusion. "Hear what?"

"Good," she said. Her eyes lingered on me for a moment as she left the bathroom.

I couldn't help but think. Sarah and Rebecca had been in the bathroom for about ten minutes before I'd started listening to their conversation. What *hadn't* I heard them say?

8

I dried my hands on my jacket and stepped out of the bathroom just as people were flooding out of the auditorium. Noah and Jonas were walking next to each other. Noah met my eyes. "Did you fall in, Haley?" he joked. I smiled, but at the same time thought *How long was I in there?* While it had only felt like a minute to me, it must have been closer to ten or fifteen.

"I hope you guys didn't miss me too much," I replied jokingly.

"I don't know how, but we managed." Jonas smiled at me. He was definitely warming to me. Noah beamed proudly and slung his arms over our shoulders. "Finally, my two best friends are acknowledging each other's existence." We all giggled together as we descended the steps of the school.

We decided to go to a local diner called Dash's Diner. Sitting in the corner of Dash's and eating greasy food, I almost felt like a normal teen. We laughed and laughed, talking about things that were in no way important but seemed so to us.

Noah leaned back against the leathery booth and finally asked what we were all thinking. "Just curious. Sorry if it's weird to ask. Did you see Rebecca and Sarah when you went to the bathroom? They never came back to the memorial."

"Uh, yeah," I replied. I couldn't lie to them, but I didn't want to mention that I'd shamelessly eavesdropped on their conversation.

Oops.

"I'm betting Rebecca was a mess?" Jonas asked.

Noah frowned and punched him in the arm. "Really, dude? She just lost her best friend. Don't be so harsh."

Jonas nodded solemnly.

"But it was weird." The words came out of my mouth before I was able to stop them, surprising me just as much as they surprised Noah and Jonas. I couldn't just leave it at that, though. It would be wrong to keep them wondering, even though I shouldn't have said anything at all.

I placed my elbows on the table and leaned forward, dropping my tone to a whisper. "Sarah and Rebecca were arguing."

Noah looked at me with newfound interest. Although he was friends with Rebecca, I could tell that from what she had told him, everything was fine between them. He popped a french fry into his mouth and, while chewing, asked, "Really? About what?"

"Sarah yelled at Rebecca and said ..." I trailed off. I felt guilty about saying anything. It felt wrong giving up details of someone else's private conversation.

Jonas leaned in, now interested. "Said what?"

"That Rebecca was obsessed with Allison."

Noah choked on his fry. "Obsessed?" He coughed to clear his throat. "Obsessed like getting a Justin Bieber tattoo, or obsessed like she wanted to be her?"

"She didn't say."

Noah shrugged and picked up another fry. "Weird. By the way, do we have any homework in English class for Monday?"

And with that, there was no discussion of Allison, Rebecca, or Sarah for the rest of the afternoon.

After a while, Noah offered to drive me home. I accepted, too tired to walk home after a long day. As soon as we got in the car, his relaxed demeanor changed. His hands gripped the steering wheel, his knuckles turning white. He closed his eyes and sighed. "Jonas and I didn't want to spoil the fun or upset you, but there's something you should know. You were going to find out eventually anyway. Mrs. Donahue announced it while you were in the bathroom. It's true. Allison was murdered."

"Oh," was all I could manage to say. For some reason, this didn't surprise me, which in itself was a bit surprising. Murder was something I knew plenty about.

And after hearing Rebecca and Sarah argue earlier that day, I wasn't so sure that Allison had had a perfect life anymore.

We drove in silence before Noah pulled up to my front door. He gave me a knowing smile. "See you, Haley."

The instant I set foot out of the car, I was hit by a wave of dread. *Something's off; something's happened.* I ran up the stone steps. When I knocked on the door, it wasn't my mother who opened it but a tall, kinda disheveled man in blue. Cops.

My heart skipped a beat. "What's wrong? Did something happen to my mom?"

"You tell me," the man said sarcastically, then motioned me to follow him. He led me to an even more horrific scene in the kitchen. My mother, a woman of few words, was nervously chatting up a pair of officers while making them coffee.

"Mom?" I interrupted. "What's going on?"

She turned around to see me and then looked at the two people sitting at our kitchen table. One man and one woman. Detectives. Both were clad in dark suits, straight out of central casting. The man had ebony skin and curly, close-cut hair. The woman was pale with angular features, an upturned nose, and dark brown hair pulled back into a severe ponytail. Neither of them smiled, but they stared straight at me. The woman seemed to be enjoying the confusion I was experiencing. The man replied for my mother. "Hi, Haley. We'd like to ask you a few questions."

"Oh, um, okay," I stammered. "About what?" I pulled out a stool and took a seat, chewing on a fingernail.

Their stares didn't falter. "About Allison Vos."

I mentally froze. After a few seconds, all I could think to say was, "She was murdered?"

Stupid, stupid, stupid. Of course she was murdered, and the officers clearly knew I knew. Everyone did now.

"Yes," said the woman. Her voice was cold, and her expression didn't change. The man, however, shifted his weight on the chair, like the thought of someone killing Allison made him uncomfortable. I wondered if the good cop, bad cop dynamic was actually a thing.

"Why are you talking to me?" I was coming out of my momentary brain freeze and was suddenly really, really curious about why they were there.

"If you don't mind, we'll be asking the rest of the questions from here. I'm Detective Marjorie Cook and this is Detective Johnathon Green."

Detective Green cleared his throat. He leaned forward with his hands clasped together and elbows on his knees. "Haley, we are aware of the situation with your father." His tone was professional but his eyes were sympathetic. It was nice to feel like I had someone on my side. I nodded.

It was Detective Cook's turn. "Were you close to Allison?" she asked.

"No, not really. I mean, we were friendly, but not friends. She was like that with everyone."

"That's interesting, because I heard that you had such nice things to say about her at her memorial." She smirked like she had caught me in a lie. She hadn't, though. I hated that she took so much satisfaction from this.

"Yeah. She was nice. Everyone seemed to like her."

"Do you have any idea as to why someone would want her dead?" asked Green softly.

"No, but as I said, we weren't close." I paused. That sounded too harsh. "I can't imagine why someone would kill her."

Cook frowned. "Well, you wouldn't know, right? You said it yourself, you didn't know her that well."

"With all due respect, Detective Cook, I was just answering the question."

A flicker of annoyance crossed her face. She folded her arms and leaned further back into her chair.

"Okay," Green said, cutting into the silence. "Let's get to it." I noticed the black satchel next to him. He shifted in his seat as he turned to pull something out of his bag. It appeared to be a stack organized neatly in a tan folder. Green shuffled the papers for a second, then looked up and smiled. "Ah-ha!" he exclaimed excitedly. Neither Cook nor I reacted. He followed suit and dropped his smile.

He continued. "Here are some of the photographs taken at the crime scene." He pushed the papers across the table so they were in my view.

My hands flew to my mouth before the gasp could even make it out of my throat. The chair I was sitting in flew backward as I shot up. Before I could run out of the kitchen, my mom blocked my path. "No, no, no," I cried.

My mother looked stern. "No, Haley." I hadn't seen this much control from her in a long time. "You need to do this."

She looked away from me and at Cook and Green. "I just need a minute with her," she told the pair of detectives as she smiled at them. They didn't smile back. She grabbed my shoulder and yanked me into the neighboring room. "Haley, you need to answer their questions."

"I can't," I sobbed. "They already think I did it."

She raised her voice. "Well, get in there and prove you didn't!" I nodded as my mother shoved me back into the room. I picked up the chair, sat down, and scooted back to the table.

I cupped my face with my hands, forcing myself to look at the photo. It was the most horrifying sight I had ever seen.

It was Allison. She was lying on the ground somewhere. Maybe her room? She was covered in blood, more blood than I had ever seen in my life, with a kitchen knife standing upright in

her chest. Her mouth and eyes were open, stuck in place, screaming forever.

To add to the horror of the scene, Allison was clutching
something in her hand.

It was a photo of Hannah with bright red X's over her eyes
and a message written on the bottom.

"Love, Dan Hansen."

"What do you want me to say?" I murmured, looking at
Cook and Green.

"Shocking, isn't it? Murder never gets easier to see. What do
you know about this?"

"What? Nothing. How could I?"

"If you did it."

I let out a noise that was half laughing, half sobbing. "If I
did it?" I wiped my nose on my sleeve and shook my head. I took
a slow breath and then started working through the shock. And
finding the anger.

"Detective Cook, if you have a minute, explain to me, slowly
and using your best big words, why I would do that to Allison.
Or anyone." I turned my head and surveyed the room. My
mother's mouth was set in a firm line, and Detective Green was
looking at me with a quizzical expression on his face, maybe even
a hint of a smile. I got the impression that he wasn't used to people talking back to Cook.

Cook pursed her lips in a tight smile. "Well, if I'm being
completely honest with you, Haley, who else would have done
it? Allison was universally beloved, filled with joie de vivre, as you
said in so many words at the memorial. So what are the odds that
someone in this town would decide to snuff that light out? And
place a picture of your best friend next to her? I can use a lot of
really great big words, but it's really a math problem, isn't it? I
subtract everyone in this town as suspects, I add a picture of Hannah to the scene, and it sort of seems to equal you, doesn't it?"
She leaned back in her chair, clearly proud of her logic.

"Hardly," I countered. "First, I have no reason to kill anyone, ever. And not many people know who I am or about my father, but some people must have their suspicions, and anyone with an internet connection can get all the details they want. Maybe you should put everyone in town with access to a computer down as a suspect." I caught a glimpse of my mom in the corner. She had a little smile playing at the corners of her mouth, a look I knew well from better times. I could only hope that it was because of me.

"She has a valid point. That being said, we do need to ask a few more questions. First, where were you early Friday morning from about four to six?" Detective Green finally said. *Thank God.* I was getting tired of his partner.

"Um …" *What?* I thought. *Sleeping like everyone else?* "I was asleep."

"Can anyone vouch for that?" asked Cook.

I looked back at my mom. "Um … I guess you could check my Life 360? It's an app that—"

"We know what it is," Cook said curtly. "I'm afraid that means nothing. Who's to say that you didn't just leave your phone at home?"

"Me."

Cook chuckled menacingly. "Well, that doesn't do you much good, now, does it?"

Green glanced at her. "We've asked enough questions for today. But we might be back to ask a few more." I nodded. Green arranged the papers and placed them back in his satchel. My mom led Green and Cook to the front door.

Cook lingered for a moment before she stepped out. "And one last thing, Haley," she said.

"Sure," I replied.

"Don't think about leaving town."

9

My mom turned to scold me the moment Cook and Green were out the door. "Are you kidding me right now, Haley?"

"What did I do?"

"You really have to tone it down. If they didn't think that you did it before, they certainly do now. You can't just go around talking to people like that, especially the police. Someday—"

"You saw how that Cook lady treated me. She thinks I did it! Nothing I say is going to change that." I couldn't believe she wasn't on my side.

"Well, you made some good points, but you could have at least tried. I swear, sometimes you act so much like your father ..." The moment the words spilled out of her mouth I could tell she regretted them. But I didn't care. At that moment I felt there was nothing I could do but walk away. "Get back here. We're not done yet. You know that's not what I meant!"

Deep down inside of me, I knew she didn't mean it. But I was afraid. If my mother could think that about me, there was no doubt in my mind that other people would think much worse.

But what scared me was that maybe she was right. Maybe I was like my father, letting my anger and resentment simmer and boil, keeping it all in until it exploded. Still, I knew I would never reach a point where I would do the things he did.

However, there was that little voice nagging in the back of my head that made me ask whether I was just telling myself that to feel better. Did my dad feel the same way right up to the point he stuck a knife in my best friend? Did my mother see in me the same madness that was buried in him?

Worse, was she afraid? Of me or for me?

Even after slamming my bedroom door, I could still hear my mother shout after me a few feet away. "Haley, open this door right now!" she screamed.

"Leave me alone!" I screamed in response. That was when the window caught my eye. I could leave right now. Cook had said that I couldn't leave town, but that didn't mean I couldn't leave my house. I threw my backpack onto the floor and started stuffing clothes inside. I didn't know where I was going, but I knew I had to leave.

My mother hadn't stopped pounding on the door. I sighed. If I left without telling her, she would surely call the police. Resigned, I opened the door to see her angry face. She was more mad and disheveled than I had ever seen her. Her grayish-blond hair was a weird mix of string and fluff, and her eyebrows seemed to be permanently scrunched up.

"I'm leaving."

"Excuse me?" she said, flabbergasted. "What do you mean, you're leaving?"

"Mom, I can't stay in this house. It's suffocating. I'll be back, but I just need a night away to clear my head."

She sighed as she slumped against the door. "Fine."

I nodded. I had to stop myself from smiling. I was genuinely surprised that she was letting me leave. I fiddled with the lock on my window and crawled out. It occurred to me that I could have just used the door, but I was in a dramatic mood.

I quickly walked down the path that led to the sidewalk in front of my house. It was starting to get dark now. Soon the street lights would turn on, illuminating the bleak streets of Fort Vepar with a golden glow.

After mindlessly walking down the street without even thinking, I ended up near the school. There was only one place to go now. I knew I couldn't sleep inside the school; that would really get tongues wagging and me expelled. That wouldn't do me any favors in the context of Allison's investigation.

I marched through the weeds and tall grass to a familiar chainmail fence. As soon as I'd jumped it, I made a beeline to the Rock. I knew that I probably couldn't sleep there, but I could at least stay there for a while. It was around eight, and I knew my mother would be asleep by ten. I could always crawl back in through the window without her noticing.

I pressed my back against the cool stone and whipped out my phone. No new messages. I sighed and hugged the phone to my chest. This was going to be a boring few hours until I could go back home unless I could find a way to kill time. I smiled as an idea popped into my head.

Question 5? Or is it 6? I don't remember. Would you rather someone always tell the truth or protect your feelings?

After a few minutes the phone buzzed, signaling his response.

question 4, actually.

Very funny, but not the answer to my question.

hhhhhmmmmm. that's a tough one. i guess i'd want people to tell the truth.

Very mysterious, care to explain why?

i don't like to be lied to.

No one does.

so haley hansen, if i'm not mistaken, you're supposed to answer the question too.

I suppose I am. I guess I'm the opposite.

you want people to lie to you?

Sometimes the truth hurts.

yeah, i guess you're right.

I was about to reply when a wave of overwhelming tiredness came crashing against me. I decided to close my eyes for a second and collect my thoughts.

The next thing I knew, something was shaking my shoulder furiously, but I was too tired to deal with it. But the shaking wouldn't stop. *"Haley, Haley, Haley,"* a voice echoed in my ear.

"What?" I murmured. I rubbed my eyes, forcing them to wake up.

"Gosh, Haley, you scared us." I looked up, still half asleep. A very concerned Noah and Jonas were crouching a few feet away from me.

"Why?" I asked, confused.

Jonas looked at me, bewildered. "Wow, Haley, I don't know. Maybe because we just found you passed out on a rock on a Monday morning."

I bolted upright. "Monday morning?" *I guess I never got home last night.* "What time is it? Like, the exact time."

"Seven thirty-one," replied Noah.

Good. At least school hadn't started yet.

I groaned and unlocked my phone. My mom hadn't even texted or called to make sure I was okay. *Lovely.*

Noah and Jonas glanced at each other and then turned back to me. "Are you going to tell us what happened, or ...?"

How can you explain? *Oh yeah, I kinda ran away from home after being interrogated by the police about a brutal murder, and my mom probably thinks I did it. Because like father, like daughter. Did I even mention that my dad brutally killed my best friend? Well, let me tell you all about it ...*

Instead, I condensed it down to the basics. "Rough night." I shrugged. It was technically not a lie.

"Most people don't fall asleep in the woods when they have a rough night," Noah said. "Well, maybe some do. But Haley, we're worried. Just tell us what happened."

I inhaled the tense air around me and slumped against the Rock. "I ran away from home."

In almost comical unison, Jonas and Noah erupted. "What?"

I chuckled. "Calm down, guys. I'll probably go home soon. I just couldn't stay at my house."

Jonas knit his eyebrows. "What happened? I mean, I know you ran away from home, but why?"

"Because the police think I killed Allison."

Noah gasped. "Oh my God. Haley, why?" His words stabbed me in the heart like a knife. The fact that he could consider that hurt just as much as him thinking that I did. Not even my mother's doubt had made me feel this bad.

My tone was flat. "You think I did it, don't you?"

Noah's face fell. "Why would you think that? I know you didn't do it."

"Then why did you ask 'why'?" I yelled. Jonas's eyes bounced back and forth like he was unsure of whose side to take.

"Ummmm," he said. "I think what Noah is trying to say is 'Why do the cops think you did it?' We know you wouldn't."

I tried to keep my breathing steady. All too often I felt like I was lashing out virtually unprovoked. How could I explain this to them without giving away too much information but not so little information that they would think I was lying? "Whoever killed her left something at the scene that they thought was mine."

"Was it?" said Noah.

Jonas frowned. "Of course it wasn't hers."

"It wasn't mine," I confirmed. "I explained that to them, but I don't think they believed me."

Noah nodded, satisfied with my explanation. I rubbed my hands through my hair. Frick, it was greasy. I hadn't had time to take a shower before I'd crawled out the window. *What am I going to do now?*

Then I realized how famished I was. I hadn't eaten anything since lunch with Jonas and Noah the day before. My stomach fluttered. "Do you have anything I could eat?" I asked them.

"Oh? Um, yeah." Jonas wrestled with his backpack to get it open. He unzipped it and handed me a granola bar. "Is there anything else we can do to help?"

"Yeah, thanks." I shoved the bar in my mouth. You never really realize how amazing food is until you're starving. "You know, come to think of it," I started, "there is something you guys can do." They smiled. "You could help me solve the murder so I don't go to jail and stuff." I had meant that as a joke, but they looked dead serious.

"Okay," said Noah.

"What?"

"I said okay," he said again. "Jonas, are you in?"

"Yeah, why not?" He shrugged.

I was shocked. "Guys, it was just a joke. How are we going to solve a murder?"

"Think about it, Haley. You said they think you did it, right?"

I nodded.

"So we need to prove them wrong, not solve a murder per se. We just need to show them that you're not the one they should be looking at."

Jonas piped up. "He's not wrong."

"Are you sure, guys? I don't want to burden you, especially with report cards and finals coming up soon. You don't owe me anything."

"Haley, we know we don't owe you anything, and we're not helping you because we have to. We're your friends. Helping you is in the job description." Noah smirked. I gave him a weak smile in return.

Friends. A warm yet bittersweet feeling filled my chest. Although I considered them my friends, I had only hoped that they considered me theirs. Ever since I'd come to Fort Vepar I had been trying to leave as little of an impression as possible on everyone I met. I seriously doubted half of my classmates even knew my name. It was nice to know that they had my back, but I was scared. The last time I had a friend, it hadn't ended too well.

"Wait, what time is it?" I asked, flustered.

Jonas looked down at his watch. "Shoot, 7:55."

Jonas and I hurried to get our backpacks and scrambled to our feet. Half tripping, we chased Noah through the trees and into the school building.

10

Most of the school day passed in a haze. I got weird looks all day. The skeptical part of my brain told me it was because they knew I was the main suspect in the investigation into the murder of our classmate, but my rational brain told me it was because I hadn't showered in two days and had slept in the woods.

I excused myself from pre-calc to freshen up. As I absent-mindedly pushed the heavy bathroom door open while checking my phone, a sudden surge of pain shot from my index finger to my knuckle. My finger had gotten stuck in the slit between the door and its frame, slowly crushing it. A primal shriek emerged from my throat. "Help! Help!" I screamed. A sophomore who was washing her hands came to my aid. As her cold, soapy hands yanked my arm out of its prison, I felt like my finger was being torn off.

"Are you okay?" the girl asked as I sank to my knees, grasping my finger. I looked down. It was contorted to the side, with a dark purple indent surrounded by a furious red. I needed to get some ice on it ASAP.

"Thanks, yeah, I'm—" I looked up at the girl. In my pain, I hadn't noticed that it was Melanie Vos. "Hey …" I started to say.

"I'm sorry," Allison's little sister blurted out as I gave her an inquisitive look. "I shouldn't have treated you so badly at the memorial."

"It's okay."

"No," she said, "it's not. It's just that before the memorial, these detectives told us that they were looking for the people that … that did this to her and they mentioned you. I know that's no excuse, but—"

"Wait," I told her. "What did they say?"

"They wanted to ask a couple of questions: If you were friends with Allison, if you had been to our house before, stuff like that. They asked about other people too, but I really don't know you, so at the memorial … I don't know what I was thinking."

"Thanks," I told her, and I meant it honestly. "Melanie, could you not mention what the detectives said about me to anyone?"

She blinked at me. "Yeah, sure. Um, do you need to go to the nurse?"

"Oh." I looked down at my finger. I had been so distracted talking to Melanie that I had completely forgotten about the throbbing sensation in my finger. Now I remembered—big time. The center of the purple blob was only getting deeper and deeper. "Yeah. Again, thanks for all your help. It means a lot to me." She nodded.

Clutching my finger, I walked down the linoleum hallway, shoes squeaking. It was oddly refreshing to walk down the empty hallway. It felt like all of the pressure of the outside world melted away and all that was left was comforting solitude.

Then I remembered where I was heading and my shoulders sagged. I dreaded going to the nurse's office. There were no redeeming qualities about it. As soon as you stepped into the stale, dank dungeon you were immediately questioned by Ms. Mulligan, an old troll of a secretary. She seriously doubted that anyone who went to the office was sick or in need of aid. If you were missing a couple of limbs, Ms. Mulligan would probably just sigh and tell you to wait on the couch for the nurse. The school nurse was very much like Ms. Mulligan. I highly doubted that she even had any medical training. The most she would do for you was give you some ice and let you wait on one of the beds until school ended.

As I suspected, this was my exact fate when I set foot in the nurse's office. "Oh my. That looks painful," the nurse said as she rotated my hand from side to side. "Probably broken, but maybe not. Take a seat on the bed over there while I get you some ice."

I grimaced in pain. My finger looked like it was melting off my hand. I sunk onto the plastic bed, but I realized I wasn't alone. Rebecca was on the other bed, just a few feet away from mine. She looked like she was in a trance. Her eyes stared straight up at the ceiling without a trace of emotion.

"Hey, Rebecca, you okay?"

"No."

"Do you want to talk about it?" I asked.

"No."

Well then. I decided to focus all my attention on my poor finger, which of course hurt even more thanks to all the interest in its well-being.

The most exciting thing to happen in the next hour was Ms. Mulligan lurching in and dropping an ice pack on my stomach. "This should work," she said, shaking her head as she looked over at Rebecca.

After what seemed like an eternity, Rebecca finally said something. "They think I did it."

"Huh?" I vocalized as I came out of my haze. "Who thinks you did what?"

"These detectives think I killed Allison."

"Did you?" I asked, somewhat hopefully, if I'm being honest. I shouldn't have said that, but Noah was right. If I wanted to clear my name, I needed to get myself out of their crosshairs. And as much as I liked Rebecca, she was as likely as anyone to have a motive.

"No," she replied.

I propped my elbow up against the bed to turn my whole body toward her. "Then why do they think you did?"

Rebecca just shrugged. "I'm not sure. I mean, we argued the night before … before she died. But that's it. It wasn't something to kill her over." She paused. "Not that I would kill anyone for anything. I'm—"

"Rebecca, Rebecca. I know," I told her. But I didn't know. *They argued the night before she died? That's more than they have on me, I guess. I didn't even know Allison and they think I might have done it.* I needed to know more. "What did you argue about?"

Rebecca still hadn't taken her eyes off of the ceiling. "Nothing important. Honestly, I can hardly remember." That was a lie if ever I'd heard one, and I'd heard quite a few doozies in my time. No one forgets the argument they had with their best friend the night before she died. I certainly didn't.

—

June 12, 2019

Hannah and I were sitting in the hammock in my backyard. It was our spot—we'd hung the hammock and planted flowers around it (with help from my dad) when we were in third grade. It was big enough to hold three people—four if you squeezed, which we had a number of times when my parents had made surprise visits on summer nights. It was underneath a cool canopy of trees, shielding us from the hot Wilake summer sun. I had closed my eyes and was enjoying the night breeze when Hannah asked out of the blue, "What do you think about Claire?"

"The one with the platinum blonde hair?"

"Yeah." I tried to lift myself with my arms to look at her, but the pressure must have unbalanced the weight on the hammock and we tipped over. I giggled and screamed as we fell. After the initial shock of the impact wore off, we shrieked with laughter. "No, but seriously, though, what do you think of Claire?"

I started to chew on my fingernail. Claire. She was the type of person everyone liked and angled to be friends with, but she wasn't my cup of tea. I thought she was a little too cheerful and overnice, if that makes sense. I could picture her in my head as a violently loud soccer mom, overwhelming people at PTA meetings.

I had made my verdict. "I don't know. Guess I'm not her biggest fan."

In annoyance, Hannah flipped her brown hair over her shoulder, although it was really too short to make any difference which only irritated me further. She looked genuinely confused. "Why do you say that?"

I continued chewing on my fingernail, mulling over my answer. "I dunno. She just kind of seems like a jerk to me."

Hannah frowned. "Just because she doesn't judge everything everyone says like you do doesn't make her a jerk," she said. "Not everyone is as stuck-up as you."

"Stuck-up?" I laughed, thinking she was joking.

"Yeah," she said. "You need to live a little, Hale. Don't be so judgmental."

"I'm not!" I suddenly didn't like the direction this conversation was going.

Hannah snorted. "You can't be serious." *What does she even mean by that?* "You just do whatever people tell you."

She was beginning to make me mad, but I knew I'd get over it. That was just what Hannah was like. She could be feisty and hurt my feelings every once in a while, but I knew she did it because she genuinely wanted to help me, never just for the heck of it.

"I'm not judgmental," I said. "Something about her just rubs me the wrong way. I get the feeling she's laughing at people behind that big smile."

Hannah started shaking her head slowly. "That's not true. I'm so sick of this freakin' superiority complex you have. You're not any better than Claire."

"But she's better than me?" I meant that as a joke. We sometimes did this—argued for no real reason with no hurt feelings later.

"Well, yeah. I guess," said Hannah. A twisting pain swirled around in my gut as if I had just swallowed a handful of needles, which were also in my brain. I had the unfortunate tendency to get raging headaches whenever I got angry or upset. Seriously, when I was little, just dropping an ice cream cone would bring on a bout of pain.

But Hannah couldn't be serious. She was my best friend. *If this is what she thinks about me, what do other people think?*

My head pounded and I gave her a blank stare. "You don't mean that."

"Not in every sense, per se," Hannah said. "She's just more exciting than you. And maybe less possessive."

I couldn't listen to this anymore. "Forget it," I said as I stormed to the edge of the backyard. I unlatched the gate and motioned for Hannah to leave. "Get out," I said. But she didn't. She just stood there, still as a statue. "Get out," I repeated, louder this time, thinking maybe she hadn't heard me.

"Haley, please, I—"

"Hannah, I honestly don't want to talk with you right now. Just leave before I say something I might regret," I yelled. "Go find Claire or something. She's much more exciting than me anyways."

"That's not what I meant," she said curtly. Deep in my heart, I knew that, but sometimes she could be so blunt that I forgot. We stood there in silence.

"I know," I told her, and I meant it. "I just need a while to cool down. See you tomorrow."

Hannah nodded. "See you tomorrow, sister. Love you." She left the yard.

And we did see each other the next day at school. And we made up and both said we were sorry. And we hugged it out. And we were happy.

But my dad didn't see that the next day. I know now, from what he said at the trial, that he watched our fight and something snapped in his mind. If he had understood real friendship, everything would have turned out differently.

That's why it's so important to take in all the little details; you might be reliving them over and over again for the rest of your life, wondering where things went wrong.

Back to the cot. The nurse's ice had helped, but it wasn't going to heal me. As nice as it was to spend a few mostly quiet hours with Rebecca, I bolted out of there when the bell rang at 3 p.m.

I placed my phone on the picnic table outside the school and used my good hand to dial my mother on speakerphone. After a few attempts, she finally picked up. "Hey, Mom, can you pick me up?"

"Ah," she said. "Coming back to the hand that feeds you."

"Actually, Mom, you don't feed me. Dad's savings do." I could hear her scoff on the other end of the phone. Maybe that was too harsh. "But you can drive."

"I'm glad I can be of service to you in some way."

"I'm sorry, Mom, I just need to get to urgent care or something. I'm pretty sure I broke my finger."

"Are you kidding me?"

"I wish I was."

She was silent for a moment. "Sweetie, urgent care's not an option. Your dad's savings only go so far," she said with a bit of snark. "I'll come get you and we can go to Walgreens to get a splint. I'll be there in a few minutes."

"Okay," I said, and hung up. I looked up. Noah was walking towards me, smiling, his hands on his backpack straps. I became conflicted. Noah was friends with Rebecca, but he was also friends with me.

Seeing as we were the only two suspects I knew about, he might have a tough time helping me try to figure out if Rebecca was a killer. "Hey," I said.

"Hey," he responded with a smile. "Have any ideas on where we should start? You know, with the case."

"Yeah," I mumbled, "but I don't think you're going to like it."

"What?" He laughed. "If you have something that could get you off the hook, then let's hear it!"

I chewed on my nail nervously. "You might not like it because—" I stopped. "Because Rebecca is the other suspect."

As I suspected, this was not welcome news to Noah. His smile immediately dropped into a frown, probably aimed at me. Maybe he had already decided that she was more valuable to him than me. "If this is a joke, it's not funny."

"It's not a joke."

"Haley, I'm trying to see how it's not a joke, but I can't. I know Rebecca. She would never do something like that." His voice started to crack. "There's no way."

He had been so quick to accept I could be a murder suspect, yet when perfect little Rebecca got into the picture—even though she was close to Allison and conceivably had more reasons to be angry with her than me—he just dismissed it out of hand. Now, why was that? I had to cool down and explain myself carefully. "I didn't think there was any way either, but when I was in the nurse's office—"

"You're not listening to what I'm saying, Haley," said Noah. "I said she didn't do it."

"No, you're not listening to me. Just let me explain myself." It was becoming difficult to keep myself composed. I inhaled sharply and released my anger with a huff. "Rebecca told me herself that she got into an argument with Allison the night before she died."

"So? Everyone gets into arguments. I argue with Jonas all the time. What was it even about?"

"That's the thing," I told him. "She said she doesn't remember."

Noah slammed his fist down on the picnic table, startling me and causing me to jump. He was starting to scare me. He must have seen it on my face, because he said, "Sorry, I'm just having a hard time processing this." But then he said, "Have you ever considered that maybe she doesn't remember what they argued about? Heck, I can't even remember what I ate for breakfast this morning."

"Okay, well, those are two completely different things. I know that if I got into an argument with my best friend the night before she died, I wouldn't forget it, no matter how small it was."

"But you don't know," Noah hissed. "You're not in her shoes. We don't know what happened."

I wasn't mad anymore, but I didn't know what I was. Resigned, maybe? My whole face felt hot and my eyes stung and I was just ... tired. Tired of pretending and walking on eggshells. *I do know*, I wanted to say. *Trust me.* But I couldn't say that. Because sometimes the truth is worse than the lie.

"Noah, you said it yourself, if I'm going to get out of this, we need to give the police some idea where to turn their attention. They're going to keep coming at me, and I don't want to be the one under suspicion for the rest of the year. It's hard enough being the new kid at school."

Noah was unable to meet my gaze. "Yeah, well, maybe I don't want to give them any ideas." And with that he walked away, leaving me standing there like an idiot.

Luckily, my mother, my new savior, pulled up at the pick-up curb. She didn't honk or roll down the window, knowing it was too risky. The news websites may not have leaked my identity, being a minor and all, but they hadn't spared my mother. She was known as the crazy lady who refused to believe that her killer husband could murder her daughter's best friend. Although she was nearly unrecognizable now, we still didn't take the risk.

At that moment, I became lost. I had no one left; not my mom, my dad, Hannah, and now not even Noah.

I went over to the tan Toyota with the scratched paint job that I still couldn't drive. I opened the door, slid into the passenger seat, and smiled at my mother; she didn't smile back. "Walgreens?" she asked, if you could even call that a question.

"Walgreens," I agreed. We drove in silence. It was clear that my mom hadn't forgiven me after the previous night's argument. I wouldn't have forgiven me either.

After a few minutes, we pulled into the parking lot and made our way through the sliding doors. Walking to the back of the store to the pharmacy aisles, I spotted an old woman studying the array of pain relievers on the shelves.

How normal her life must be, I thought. She was short, with wiry gray hair and smile lines. She had probably never been involved in a murder investigation. Sure, she would have lost many important people in her life by now, but perhaps not in the same spectacular fashion as I had. For the first time in my life, I found myself desperately wishing I was an elderly woman. Most of her life was in the past, and now, toward the end, she was left standing. *If only I could be so lucky.* I snapped out of it. *Time to focus on the here and now, Haley.* And my first priority was picking out a finger splint that could magically replace the need for a doctor and X-rays.

My mother was waiting for me near the cash register, her permanent scowl plastered on her face. She was clutching a few of the necessities in a shopping cart: boxed mac and cheese, cigarettes, and a liter bottle of Fanta so orange it made my stomach lurch.

After paying, we made our way back to the car. I thought the ride back home would be more of the same sullen silence, but my mouth suddenly moved without permission from my brain. "Mom, are you happy here?"

She glanced over at me. "Well, aren't you talkative today?" she snapped. "Why do you ask stuff like that?"

I shrugged. "I was just thinking, you know, we might be better off somewhere else."

Her scowl remained, but she let out a sigh. "What makes you think we'd be happier someplace else? Fort Vepar is as good as we'll get. We can't leave town now anyway, according to the cops. But once this clears up, I don't feel like running anymore. Running's expensive."

Neither of us said anything for a bit. My mom finally cleared her throat and glanced over at me, one eye on the road. "Did you get yourself in more trouble? If so, just tell me now." *More trouble? What did I do in the first place?* She didn't say anything else, but her silence spoke volumes. My mother thought I was like my father and accepted the possibility that I could be a cold-hearted killer too.

"No, Mom. I didn't do anything."

"Then why are you in such a rush to get out of here?"

"Because I'm alone." For the first time in the past six months, my mother didn't have a sarcastic comeback or deflect anything. "Let's not pretend, Mom. We don't exactly have the best relationship." She opened her mouth as if she were about to refute that, then slowly seemed to accept what I was saying.

"Not a day goes by where we don't ignore each other's existence or get into an argument. So I can't exactly talk to you. My best friend thinks I killed Allison and probably never wants to talk to me again. Oh, and let's not forget about Dad. Actually, yes. Let's forget about Dad, because we never even talk about him. You can't just pretend that nothing happened, Mom, that we're okay."

Fat tears streamed down her face. She pulled the car over into our driveway but made no indication that she was leaving it.

"Oh, Haley ..." she said. She sniffed as she wiped the tears from her eyes. "I've been such a bad mother to you."

"I shouldn't have said anything," I stammered, immediately trying to put everything back in the bottle.

"I'm trying, Haley. I am. It's hard for me too, you know?"

I nodded.

"But I know that sometimes I need to try harder, to be a better mother for you. I'll put the effort in. I'll get a job. I promise."

I doubted there was much truth in what she was saying, but I leaned in for a hug anyway. She gripped me tight, too tight, like she was trying to stop me from jumping out of the car and leaving her forever. It was surprising how much strength she had in that willowy frame. I suppose it's the kind of strength that mothers can summon if they think their kids are in mortal danger. She sniffled one last time before letting me go. "Help me with the bags, will ya?"

"Of course," I said.

11

Our highly emotional Walgreens trip wore my mother out; she was asleep no more than five minutes after we walked into the house.

I, on the other hand, had important business to attend to—finding out who killed Allison and why. I sat on my bed and started making a list of everything I knew on Post-it notes so I could stick them to my wall. It made me feel like all these random thoughts weren't just rattling around inside my head. Writing them down brought them into the real world.

So what do I know? I knew that Allison was well-liked, at least on the surface. She'd gotten into an argument with Rebecca the night before she died, and Rebecca wouldn't say why. And Sarah didn't seem too concerned that her best friend had been murdered, which had caused Rebecca and Sarah to get into an argument at the memorial. What did Sarah say to Rebecca again? Oh yeah, "You were obsessed with her." But Rebecca didn't strike me as the obsessive type.

I was just about to stick the notes on the wall above my desk when my phone buzzed again. *Huh?* Maybe it was Noah to apologize for earlier, but I highly doubted that. Noah didn't usually get into conflicts, but when he did, he was stubborn.

It was Jonas.

question 5, what did you do to piss off Noah?

Glad to see you semi-using punctuation, but what kind of question is that?

the one i should be asking.

I grunted. If there was one thing I couldn't stand, it was nosy people. It was none of his business.

If you must know, I actually found something that could be helpful to Allison's case, but Noah no longer wants anything to do with me.

i find that hard to believe, you're going to need to fill in some gaps

I told him that Rebecca and Allison had argued the night before she'd died. Also that Rebecca might have done it.

Little dots appeared and disappeared while Jonas was typing. It was taking him a long time to respond. I couldn't blame him. I didn't know what I'd say to myself. Probably something along the lines of "Nice going, Haley, you screwed up again!" Finally, the little dots turned into a bubble.

yikes. that's just because Noah's a little biased. he'll come around eventually.

Biased? How so?

The more I thought about it, this whole blow-up with Noah was perplexing. Rebecca and Noah were friends, sure, but only casually and, it seemed, fairly recently. It wasn't like they were best friends.

But then a curveball.

Jonas: are you kidding? he's been in love with Rebecca since freshman year.

Of course he was. Wasn't it obvious? How could I have been so stupid?

Interesting. Whether he likes her or not, he's still not talking to me or helping with the case.

i guess we'll just have to do a little more work.

We?

uh oh, have i been dropped?

Of course not. I just assumed that you didn't want to help me, because, you know, Noah.

i'm not just Noah's friend, i'm yours too.

Thanks.

you don't have to thank me.

Well, I just did. Do you want to come over tomorrow and work on the case?

yeah, i'll see what i can find.

Thank you, see you tomorrow.

no haley, thank you.

Then he went offline. My heart fluttered. Whatever happened next, at least I wasn't going solo.

12

The next day, time moved … so … slowly. I'd lived in Fort Vepar for six months and virtually nothing had changed except the weather. Now, all of a sudden, it was like my life was in hyperdrive, just as it had been after Hannah died. So I can't say I was terribly disappointed that my life had returned to the dull. But still, we had a murder to solve.

Near the end of class, I found myself checking the time every few minutes on my plastic flower watch, hoping that glaring at the watch would make time move faster. Spoiler alert: it didn't.

There was only one thing on my mind all day: Jonas. I was looking forward to our little sleuthing mission after school. The previous night, I had completely slacked off. I knew I probably should have put a little more effort into the crime wall, but my mind was too scrambled. As I tried to sleep or concentrate on the case, I kept replaying the day's events over and over again. The good things: texting with Jonas and reconciling with my mom. The bad things: losing Noah and almost my finger.

After what seemed like an eternity in physics class, the clock finally struck three. I lagged behind after the bell, partly because I didn't want to get caught in the stampede of students. After stuffing my backpack, I ambled to the picnic table where I had argued with Noah the day before.

The table was almost visible from the entrance of the school. Getting there only required a short walk to the right of the building. Jonas was waiting there for me. And so was Noah.

They seemed involved in a deep conversation, although I could tell that Jonas was trying to back out of it. He brushed his dark hair off his pale face absentmindedly, occasionally glancing at his phone.

Almost here, I texted him. Jonas looked straight up and then turned his head to the left, meeting my gaze. He smiled at me. Noah followed suit and looked up at me as well, but he had a different reaction. He stood abruptly, almost angrily, and gave Jonas a playful salute, as if to signal goodbye. He then trudged off along the longer path to the school, all without meeting my eyes. *Probably for a tutoring session with Rebecca*, I thought.

"Let me guess," I told Jonas, "he's still mad at me."

"Your guess is correct," he said as he stood up. He nudged his head in the direction of my house as if to say "Are you ready?" I nodded in response. We shared a silent method of communication. Even though I had only really gotten to know Jonas in the past few days, I felt comfortable around him. As we walked off towards my house, Jonas said, "He's meeting with Rebecca, you know."

I sighed. "I expected as much. Tutoring?"

"He didn't say." Paranoia crept through my veins. Was it possible that Noah and Rebecca were plotting against me? I'd never thought of Noah or Rebecca as that kind of person, but if the last few days had taught me anything, it was that people aren't what they seem, and all bets are off in a situation like this. "Have you heard anything back from the detectives?"

I shook my head. "No." Maybe I hadn't heard from them in the past few days, but then I remembered—they had shown me pictures of the crime scene. "By the way, I forgot to mention something. While the detectives were at my house, they showed me pictures of the crime scene and stuff. Also the time it happened."

Jonas sighed contentedly. "That's a lot of information, Haley. We're in a lot better shape than I thought." I must have looked guilty, because he said, "Don't worry, Haley. This is a good thing."

"I have to admit something else," I said slyly.

"My interest is piqued. Do tell, Haley. What other secrets are you hiding?" I had to catch my breath. What a question. *What secrets am I hiding? If only he knew.* I knew that he was just making a joke, but I couldn't help but feel guilty. We'd have a much easier time solving the case if I told him about my father. And what the killer had left at the crime scene.

"I made a murder board."

Jonas let out a deep belly laugh. "A murder board? Like the kind you see in British murder mysteries and cheesy Hallmark movies?"

"Exactly like you see in British murder mysteries and cheesy Hallmark movies."

"Haley Hansen, the soul of a sixty-year-old British man and the appearance of an American sixteen-year-old girl," Jonas joked. "So, what exactly is on this 'murder board'?"

"Just the usual crime stuff," I teased him. "I'm working on writing down everything I know—well, knew—about Allison. And what I know happened leading up to her death," I explained. "We should probably start by working on some sort of timeline of events and 'clues,' if you will."

"Sounds good to me," he said. His phone buzzed in his pocket. He stopped walking momentarily to fish around for it before eventually retrieving it. He looked down and scowled at it. "That's weird."

I stopped walking too. "What is?"

"Noah wants me to call him. Do you mind if I take this?"

I shook my head. That didn't seem weird at all. But then I realized it probably was. Noah wasn't much of a caller. Who was, these days? He much preferred texting or snapping.

"What's up?" Jonas asked Noah on the phone, then grimaced. "What?" I couldn't make out what Noah was saying at the other end, but I could tell he was saying it urgently.

"Yeah, I still don't understand," said Jonas. Noah's voice got louder. This must be bad. Noah rarely raised his voice. "Uh, yeah. Okay, we'll be right there."

"What is it?" I asked. "We'll be right there?"

"Yeah. Noah needs us to go back to school. He says Rebecca wants to talk to you. He said to meet at the Rock."

"What? Why?" So he had shown Rebecca the Rock. It looked like he was already filling the social void that the loss of our friendship had caused.

Jonas shrugged. "I'm not sure, but Noah says it's urgent. Something about what the cops said to Rebecca."

I inhaled sharply. The cops must have spoken to Rebecca again. About me. Why else would she need to talk to me? But I was still so confused. They hadn't talked to me again, but why? Didn't they trust that I would tell them the truth? Or did they think I was guilty and they were just tightening the noose?

"Well, I guess we should head over, then," I managed. Jonas and I turned around and started walking back towards the Rock. *Might be home a little later, with friends*, I texted my mom. The last thing I needed now was for her to start worrying. We didn't talk much on the way to the Rock, or at least I didn't. Our communication mostly consisted of Jonas asking me questions and me responding to those questions by nodding or shaking my head. I think I might have thrown in a noncommittal shrug here and there.

As we got closer, Jonas put his hand on my shoulder. "Hey, Haley." His hand was comforting, conveying more to me than words could. "Don't be so worried. Loosen up." I had to fight back a laugh. That was exactly what Hannah had told me. *You need to loosen up.* "Whatever Rebecca has to say to you, it's probably nothing. You've seen how she's been the last few days. To say that she's a mess is an understatement." I didn't say anything back. I just nodded. "Hey, look at me," said Jonas. He placed his other hand on my shoulder and turned me so that I was looking at him. "Shake it out."

I giggled. "Shake it out?" I repeated.

He broke away from me and took a few steps back. "Shake it out," he said again. Then he did the thing I least expected to see someone like Jonas do. He danced. Well, not exactly dancing. It was some sort of strange body wiggle. Like a jellyfish. His arms shook with no easily identifiable pattern. His legs moved back and forth in a shimmy, you could say.

I was laughing so hard that I sank to the ground on my knees with a hand on my chest. After about a minute or so of this, Jonas stopped, giving me, the audience, a quick bow. "Now you try it."

"Me?" I asked, a ridiculously large grin on my face.

He took my hands. "Yes, you." He began to move from side to side, forcing me to shake along with him. I couldn't help it, I laughed and I laughed and then I wiggled. A minute later, I was so out of breath that I hugged Jonas to get him to stop moving. His body tensed up, then his muscles relaxed as he returned the hug.

We pulled apart. "Are you ready now?" he asked. I nodded, still smiling, as we hiked to the all-too-familiar clearing.

13

Rebecca was sitting on my rock. *Our rock.* I don't know why this made me so mad, but it did. Maybe it was because I felt so easily replaced.

But then it occurred to me, Noah *couldn't replace me.* Not as long as Jonas and I were friends. It was *him* who might be replaced. Whether I was jealous or not, Rebecca was still sitting on my rock across from Noah. Her legs were crossed, with her arms wrapped around them, securing them tight to her chest.

Although I was mad, I felt bad for Rebecca. She looked worn down and weathered, almost like my mother.

"Hey," said Jonas as we climbed over the fence to the stream.

Noah hopped off the Rock. "Hey." He motioned to Rebecca. "She wants to talk to Haley."

"Yeah, I got that." They stood there staring each other down. It was almost like they were in the middle of a standoff, each trying to get some sort of point across to the other. I cleared my throat, breaking the silence.

"Shall we?" I asked Rebecca.

"Sure," she replied with a quivering lip. She looked shaken up just by my presence. *Is she scared of me?* I wondered. She didn't have a reason to be.

"Over there?" she asked. She pointed to a log a little way up the stream. It would be in Jonas and Noah's line of sight but just out of earshot.

"Okay," I replied. Noah eyed me skeptically as Rebecca and I trudged over to the log. It was muddy, and I constantly lost my balance walking over fallen sticks and branches. I regretted not picking an easier spot.

Finally, we made it to the log. I could practically feel Noah's eyes burning into the back of my neck as if he was waiting for me to screw up so that he could swoop in and save Rebecca. At that moment, I almost resented him.

I placed my hoodie on the damp rock, although it seemed silly. Getting a wet butt print on the back of my jeans was the least of my worries right now. Nevertheless, I did this, perhaps in an attempt to gain some feeling of normalcy, like Rebecca wasn't about to accuse me of murdering her best friend.

I patted the space next to me, motioning Rebecca to sit down. She did so hesitantly. "So you wanted to talk?"

"Yeah," she said. But she wouldn't look at me. Her eyes were focused downward, on the fingernails she was picking at. It looked like she had been doing that a lot in the past few days. They were about half the size they should have been, with ragged edges. They looked so out of place on Rebecca, who, despite the tragedies of the past few days and the mournful look she wore on her face, was beautiful. Her button nose and deep brown eyes complemented her chocolate hair and ochre skin perfectly. Although she was often viewed as "less" than Allison and Sarah, she still looked like she could be a model. No wonder Noah was apparently in love with her. "So the cops talked to me again yesterday."

I acted surprised, not wanting to be rude even though this was a piece of information I already had. "So what did they say?"

Rebecca hesitated before she spoke, like she knew she was about to say something she would regret. The words finally seemed to come to her. "So those detectives ... Green and Cook, I think? They asked me if I knew who Dan Hansen was."

My hands flew to my eyes. How was everyone finding out about my father? "Rebecca, could you not tell—"

"Let me finish," Rebecca said sternly. My mouth hung open in shock. Even before Allison died, I had never seen Rebecca have the confidence to stand up for herself like that. "So I said 'No' and they were like 'Are you sure? Because this was found at the crime scene.'" She paused for a moment. "Then they showed me this picture, and I swear, Haley, it was the most disgusting thing I have ever seen."

"I know," I lamented. "They showed it to me too." She gave me a sympathetic smile. "Pretty horrifying, right?"

Rebecca nodded. "So anyways, the detectives looked confused when I said I didn't know who that was. And that mean lady, Cook, was like 'Think carefully,' so I did. Then I thought *Wait a minute—Dan Hansen, Hansen, Haley Hansen*." She went back to picking at her nails for a moment, but she seemed less nervous than she had a few minutes ago. It must be a relief, I thought, to be able to get so much off your chest without facing major consequences. "So they told me who Dan Hansen is, and I just wanted to hear it from you, Haley. Who is he?"

"He's my dad," I confessed. It was painful to think about, even more painful to vocalize. "A few months ago, he killed my best friend, Hannah, and now he's in prison for the foreseeable future." Hot tears began to sting my eyelids, but I looked up, trying to drain them. "And the worst part about it is, other than the obvious fact that my best friend is dead, is that he still thinks he did the right thing. And we have to live here. Away from everything I've ever known because my entire town thinks it's my fault."

"Haley, it's okay," Rebecca reassured me.

There was no stopping me now. The secrets I had been keeping from everyone in the past few months began to flow out of me. Like someone had broken down the dam of my emotions, they could no longer be tamed. They raged like uncontrollable gushing water. "You probably think I did it too. And so does my mother. I can't even protest or say that I'm innocent because then it just makes me look more guilty, and there's nothing I can do to change anyone's mind."

"Haley, stop it. You're not listening to me. No one does. I don't think you did it."

"You don't?"

"No, of course I don't, but Cook and Green do. That's why I wanted to talk to you. What I wanted to do is warn you."

"Warn me?" I asked.

"Yes. As I said, Cook and Green think you did it. We know you didn't. It's obvious you don't have it in you. I'm happy that they're not looking at me anymore, but I want justice for Allison. I don't think I could live with myself if I just let an innocent person take the fall for what happened to clear my name." She put her hand on my shoulder, comforting me just like Jonas had. "I want to help you, Haley, and Noah will too. Once we explain to him—"

"Thank you, Rebecca, but I don't think we should tell anyone about my dad," I interrupted. I had to make that clear right off the bat. Rebecca nodded, but I could see other possibilities dancing across her eyes like she was considering whether to take me seriously or not. "Rebecca, I'm dead serious, more for my mother than for me. This is the only place she feels semi-comfortable, and we can't afford to move right now."

I paused for a second to think of a way to seal the deal. "Eventually my name will get leaked to the press. So even if you think we're just telling a few people, we're actually telling the whole world." I could only hope that that would stick.

"Okay," she decided after a few moments. "But I get to help. And so does Noah."

I froze. "Noah?"

"Yes, Noah. I can tell he's important to you, Haley. You need him, and he needs you."

I snorted. "No, Rebecca, he needs you. When push comes to shove, Noah's always going to choose you over me."

Rebecca knitted her brows, confused. "What do you mean?"

"I just thought—well, Jonas told me—Noah has a thing for you. Always has," I said shyly. I felt bad, like I had just exposed a huge secret. I had just assumed that Rebecca already knew.

Rebecca just picked her nails without saying a single word.

"Well, do you have feelings for him?"

"Well, no. Not exactly. I mean, I like him as a friend, but that's it. I've never felt anything else."

"I'm sorry I brought it up. Is it okay if we don't mention this to Noah?"

Rebecca let out a dry laugh. "Please. I wouldn't mind that at all, under one condition—you give Noah a second chance."

"Fine. Do you two want to join me and Jonas to work on the case? Sarah too, if you think that's something she'd be interested in."

"Sure," she said with a weak smile. "But not Sarah. She and I ... we're not exactly friends anymore. Shall we head back to the boys?"

I nodded in response and we stood up. I brushed off the mud and twigs that had stuck to my hoodie while we were sitting on the log. We walked back through the damp forest toward Jonas and Noah.

"What's the update?" shouted Jonas with his hands on both sides of his mouth.

"We've decided the best option for me is to cross the border to Canada and hide there until my name is cleared," I said, but Noah and Jonas looked perplexed. "Jesus, I'm joking. Rebecca and Noah are going to help us with the case."

Noah looked at Rebecca with his head tilted to the side, as if to say *what?* "We are," Rebecca confirmed. "And we're going to Haley's to work on it." Noah nodded. It was clear that whatever Rebecca said, he'd agree with her. Heck, he'd jump off a cliff if she told him to. For the second time that day, Jonas and I went to my house with Rebecca and Noah in tow.

14

Bringing some friends over, don't freak out, I texted my mom. Little bubbles appeared and disappeared on the left of the screen while I waited for her reply.

OK, she texted back. *Be careful.* I knew she would be wary of me inviting people over. She was petrified of people recognizing her, which was why she seldom left the house, and then only at odd hours. Rebecca already knew who we were, and I highly doubted Jonas or Noah would recognize her.

We walked up the steps and I knocked on the door. "Mom," I called.

"Come in," she replied in a whispery voice. I opened the door. She stood there leaning against the living room wall, looking like she was deciding if she should pull a runner or not. I could tell that she didn't like this, but she didn't want to upset me after our argument.

Noah just blinked at her curiously, but Rebecca and Jonas both gave me an understanding look.

"She looks just like you," Jonas said once my mother was out of earshot. I had to swallow my retort. I knew Jonas meant that as a compliment. After all, my mother was once beautiful. But I didn't want to think that we were similar in any way.

"This way," I said and led them to my room. The door was stuck on the carpet and I had to give it a body slam to get it open.

They were all silent as they surveyed the room, soaking up my minimalist approach to interior decorating. Not a poster on the

69

wall or any indication that this room belonged to me. The only pieces of furniture in the room were my bed and desk, a picture of Hannah and me when we were eight on the bare desk, the box of journals in the corner, and the Post-it notes stuck to the wall.

"Well," said Noah to break the silence, "shall we get started?"

"Yup," replied Jonas. We all threw our backpacks into the corner. Jonas took a seat on my bed and Rebecca at my desk, while Noah stood there awkwardly. They were all reading the Post-it notes I had put up the night before. *Frick.* I hadn't removed the one about Rebecca, but she didn't seem to notice.

"I'll start," Rebecca volunteered. "Allison hadn't been acting weird before she died. She was normal, I guess." Rebecca paused. "Now that I think of it, Allison *was* acting weird—more distant, and it seemed to get worse the Thursday before she died."

"Is that what you argued about?" I asked. Noah scowled at me. He probably didn't appreciate me bringing up what was clearly a sore subject for Rebecca.

"Sort of," Rebecca said. She didn't bother to add any more detail. I couldn't help but think that we would have a much easier time solving this if we were all completely honest with each other. But then again, that was hypocritical of me. I couldn't tell Noah and Jonas about my father, or anyone, for that matter. We all had our secrets. No one wanted to share them, but everyone wanted to know them.

I tossed my stack of Post-it notes to Rebecca. "Write that down and stick it to the wall. Who's next?"

"Might as well be you," said Jonas. "Didn't you say that the detectives showed you a picture of the crime scene or something?"

Rebecca and I made eye contact. "Uh, yeah," I stammered. "We both saw it." Rebecca nodded at me as if to say *Your dad, your story*. I wasn't sure how to describe it without giving away too much information. I decided to be completely honest with them but stop myself when I was about to say too much.

"So, it was pretty gruesome. I don't know why they showed it to us except maybe to shock a confession out of one of us," I speculated. "She was in her room, I think—was it her room, Rebecca?" Rebecca nodded. "Okay, so she was in her room, on the ground. Lots of blood. Someone stabbed her with a kitchen knife or something similar sometime early Friday morning. They think."

No one spoke. Even if this was our new normal, it didn't mean that it wasn't difficult to hear the bloody details of the death of a person we'd known living and breathing just days before. "Anything else?" asked Noah.

"Yeah. Allison's killer left something with her—a photograph."

"Of what?" Noah asked, sarcasm edging its way into his voice. Rebecca kicked him in the knee, which made him blush. It disgusted me how desperate he was for her attention.

Here was where things were bound to get a little dodgy. I wasn't sure how we could go down this path without Jonas and Noah assuming I was guilty or at least in the know about what had happened. They'd be fools not to, actually.

I tried a little evasion, thinking it through while tossing more Post-it notes to Noah. "Make sure to write everything down."

"Don't change the subject, Haley. What was the photograph of?" asked Noah. He was beginning to annoy me.

"Fine. It was a photograph of some girl that got killed last year." It pained me to have to refer to Hannah as "some girl," because really, she was so much more. They all eyed me, waiting for more. "At the bottom of the photo—it was a Polaroid, so it had that white part—it said 'Love, Dan Hansen.' That's the guy that killed her. Oh, and her eyes were covered with X's too."

They all looked at me, saying nothing. "Hansen? By chance any relation to Haley Hansen?" asked Jonas.

I shook my head *no*. "Nope. Weird, but just a coincidence."

"Strange," said Noah. "I don't understand. Why leave a picture of a dead girl at the scene of another murder? It's not like they knew each other, right?"

71

"I don't think so," said Rebecca. She was right. Hannah didn't know what Fort Vepar was or where it was. No one did. It was highly unlikely that they had ever met. If they had, Hannah would have told me. "Do we have anything else?"

"Well, we know what happened. But we have no clue who or why," said Noah. "We're still missing, like, eighty percent of what we need to know."

"Rebecca, you guys were close," I said gently. "Did you know of anyone who would have wanted to hurt Allison? Like, did she have some kind of blood feud with anyone?"

Rebecca stared into space and picked at her nails. "There are only two things I can think of. That week she was on her phone a lot, texting someone. But she wouldn't say who. And she and Sarah all of a sudden weren't getting along very well."

"Why do you think that is?" asked Jonas.

Rebecca shrugged. "I'm not sure, so I can only guess. The best I can think of is that Sarah was jealous of Allison. Like, crazy jealous. Sometimes I think that Sarah wasn't friends with Allison, she was friends with Allison's popularity."

"Jealous enough to kill her?" asked Jonas. Rebecca seemed annoyed by this, but it was what we all were thinking. If Jonas hadn't asked it, I would have.

Rebecca looked down, shaking her head. "Sorry, guys, it's just … I'm having a hard time wrapping my head around all of this. You guys didn't really know Allison. Everyone has an idea of who Allison was, but no one has it right. Everyone thinks she was this perfect person, but she wasn't. She was flawed." Rebecca chuckled dryly. "We all are, right? What most people didn't see was that Allison was so anxious. She worried about anything and everything. Whenever she thought she'd made a mistake, it would just break her. I think that's why she stuck with Sarah for so long. She gave her guidance and reassured her that she was doing the right thing."

All was silent for a few moments. Rebecca had been talking for so long that we expected her to say more. After a while, I had to ask the question that was on all of our minds. "Did she ever confide in you like she did in Sarah?"

"Sometimes," said Rebecca, sadness edging its way into her voice. "Sometimes Allison would break down and say everything was a mistake."

"A mistake? But everyone loved Allison." Noah's brow was furrowed.

"Yeah, well, she couldn't see that. She wanted everything to be different, which annoyed Sarah. Sometimes I think she felt that Sarah and I were the mistakes."

15

That really sucked the air out of the room. We finished Post-it noting everything and stuck them to my wall. After some talks about our next steps, they all went home. It was getting latish, about seven o'clock.

Looking at the board in the quiet of my room, I realized it was an odd jumble of things. I wanted to be able to take a string and connect everything together like they did in the movies, but I just couldn't make sense of it all. I wasn't getting that *ah-ha!* moment. So I took a stab at my homework but soon found myself bored out of my mind. I eventually succumbed to checking my social feed. As I scrolled through posts, it seemed as though everyone in town had already moved on from Allison's death. Every inane discussion was exactly what it had been a week ago. From the outside looking in, you wouldn't be able to tell that anything had changed. The thought of how short our collective attention span was made me overwhelmingly sad for a moment, but then I remembered how it had worked out for me—Dan Hansen was a media sensation for a hot minute, but then the world moved on, leaving my mother and me to collect up the pieces of our broken lives.

Kinda heavy, man. But soon my eyelids grew heavy from struggling with all this, and I drifted off as a black curtain drifted down over my mind.

I went into the kitchen to get something to eat and check in with my mom but came up short. Instead of my perpetually frazzled mom, it was Cook and Green sitting at our circular kitchen table.

They wore the same suits as when we'd first met, and despite the early hour, they didn't seem tired at all. I wondered how they did it.

"Well, good morning, Haley. Time to talk," said Cook in a condescending tone. I hated that she thought she was the puppet master and I was the puppet. But, in general, I just hated her.

"Nice to see you again," I replied. I pulled up a chair and eased myself into it like we were old friends about to enjoy a casual breakfast together.

Green smiled at me, but unlike Cook, there was nothing malicious behind it. "Nice to see you too, Haley. As you've probably guessed, we're just here to ask a few more questions. You have nothing to be nervous about. This is completely routine."

Routine, my ass. "Okay," I said, trying to look as nonchalant and personable as possible.

"Great," he said. "Let's get started." He bent over to grab something from his satchel and pulled out a fun-sized handheld recorder. He must have seen me eyeing the box warily, because he reassured me, "We just want to record our conversation so we don't have to keep asking the same questions, all right?" He cleared his throat. "Detective Green and Detective Cook commencing the interview with Haley Hansen at ..." He looked down at his watch. "Seven-fourteen, Wednesday, November 13, 2019."

"Haley, have you had contact with your father recently?" Cook asked abruptly.

This caught me off guard. I had presumed that the questioning would be about Allison. "No," I stammered. "I haven't spoken with him since about a week after his arrest."

"And prison records confirm this?" asked Cook. I nodded. "Verbally, please, for the recording."

"Yes," I confirmed.

"And what did you discuss during this visit?" she inquired.

"I don't fully remember," I told her, and the tape recorder too, of course. "I guess I just wanted to ask him why he did it." I was starting to feel like Cook and Green were my very aggressive therapists.

"Do you remember exactly what you asked him and how long your visit was? I find it difficult to believe that you don't remember the last time you saw your father," she implied, a little more forcefully this time. I wished Green was asking the questions.

"Probably something along the lines of 'Why did you kill my best friend and ruin Mom and my lives?'" I paused. "Sorry, that came out worse than I thought, but I probably did ask something like that. The visit couldn't have lasted more than a few minutes. I wasn't exactly dying to get to talk to him." *Nice choice of words, Haley.*

"And what was your dad's response?" asked Green softly.

I inhaled. "He said he did it for me, but I can't see how. He said that Hannah was corrupting me and hurting me, but she wasn't." The pair looked at me, expecting me to say more, but I didn't know what else to say. All I could do was keep talking and hope nothing I said sounded too guilty, even if it was the truth. "I guess he thought Hannah was dishonest. That was one thing he could never stand. I knew he hadn't liked Hannah for a while, but I never expected him to go that far."

"Haley, I'm assuming you are aware of the following that your father has attracted."

I nodded, then, catching myself, said "Yes."

For. The. Recorder.

"And how does that make you feel?" asked Green.

"Sick. I can't tell if people look up to him or are fixated on him because what he did and why he did it are so bizarre. It's often a blurred line, fixation and admiration."

"And where do you fall on that line, Haley, of fixation and admiration?" Cook asked. Green shifted in his seat uncomfortably. There was something about him that told me that he hadn't been in this career for long. Like the idea that he could be interviewing the killer seemed foreign to him.

Cook's question irritated me. "I'm not on the line," I told them. "I detest my father. I'm neither fixated on him nor do I admire him."

"Now let's talk about Allison," she said. I groaned tiredly. I hoped the tape didn't catch that. I knew that this would all have to loop back to her somehow. I just didn't know how.

"Did she remind you of Hannah?"

What? How was I supposed to answer that? I barely knew Allison, and Hannah was my best friend. Cook just wanted me to say yes, looking for a motive where there was none. But I couldn't lie to her, because she was right. In a way, Allison did remind me of Hannah.

"Kind of. Like I've said before, I didn't know Allison that well. But she and Hannah were nice and extroverted, so I guess."

Green and Cook looked at each other. "Okay, only a few more questions. You're doing great," Green added encouragingly. I smiled.

"Towards the end of her life, did you resent Hannah?" inquired Cook. I dropped my smile. What was the point of trying to make me relive all this? Hannah hadn't even known Allison.

"Of course not. She was my best friend," I replied.

Green looked at Cook. "I think that's enough for today, don't you think?" Cook nodded hesitantly. Green leaned forward and spoke into the metal box. "Questioning terminated at seven twenty-seven." He placed the tape recorder back into his satchel. "Thanks, Haley. We'll be in contact. If you have any questions or need to tell us anything, you can call this number." He scribbled it down on the back of a receipt that was lying on the kitchen counter and handed it to me with a smile. He and Cook stood up and left the house.

I let out a deep breath. *Finally.*

Then it occurred to me: I was going to be late for school unless I left in the next five minutes. No time for breakfast. I sprinted into my room and got dressed in a hurry, throwing on a large T-shirt and a pair of leggings that I was ninety percent sure didn't match. I looked around furiously, trying to remember what I needed for school that day.

Something seemed off about my room, but I couldn't quite put my finger on it. I looked around. At first glance, it was impossible to tell if anything had changed, but at second glance, there was a change so jarring I couldn't believe I hadn't noticed it before. The picture of Hannah and me was gone, leaving my desk depressingly blank. There was no time to think about this. I needed to leave ASAP.

My heart was beating too rapidly and I couldn't think straight. I passed over the room like a tornado, putting everything in sight into my old backpack. I bolted out the door, giving my dazed mother a hurried goodbye, a question on the tip of her tongue.

7:35. About a block in, I stopped to catch my breath. The school was only a few minutes' walk away. I was going to make it if I kept running. Time for another exciting day at Fort Vepar High School. Sigh.

Despite seemingly packing everything in sight into my backpack, I found myself wildly unprepared for the school day. When I slid into the seat next to Noah for biology and tried to get my textbook out in preparation for a lab, I found it missing. I cursed under my breath, attracting the attention of a couple of nosy classmates. Noah flashed me a curious look. "Can't find my book. Can we share?" I whispered.

Noah nodded and whispered, "Just pull out another one so Mr. Carlouci doesn't catch on." Our biology teacher was known to have no mercy on those who came to class unprepared. I gave him a thumbs-up and reached into my backpack to pull out a replacement book that was similar in size. To my surprise, it was one of the journals that I hadn't bothered to put away a few days ago. I wasn't sure how it had ended up in my backpack.

From what I could tell, this was one of the journals I hadn't yet removed from the box. It was my father's, one I hadn't bothered to look at before. I turned it to a random page and placed it on the table next to Noah's textbook.

As Mr. Carlouci droned on and on about the scientific method and proper safety techniques, I got more and more curious about the journal. My eyes drifted to its pages. It wasn't too old, probably from the last two years or so. From what I could tell, the writing in the journals wasn't the usual paragraphs about what my dad had eaten for dinner or what he did during the day. It was more of a list of semi-incoherent thoughts. Despite this, the journal was pretty organized. The notes were sorted by months and years, with each month taking up a few pages. I started with an entry dating back to December 2018, six months before Hannah died.

Haley cut hair. To look more like Hannah? Why so close?

Saw Haley put on eyeshadow today.

Faith acting weird for her. Making more family dinners, takes effort to get Haley there. Why can't that kid sit down with us?

Haley talking to Faith less, makes her sad.

Faith spending too much time on computer. Apparently not for family.

Was work always this boring?

Faith and Haley not the same anymore. Everything changing around me. Makes me scared.

It was odd. I hadn't necessarily been thinking of anything before reading the list, but this unsettled me way more than a fully written paragraph could. Although I was scared of what the rest of the lists would look like, I couldn't stop myself from reading them. Luckily, we were flipping pages in our textbooks, and I flipped to February 2019.

Told Haley and Faith was going to New York for a work trip.

Sitting in hotel room, feeling nothing. Didn't attend meetings.

Looked at Haley and Hannah's instagrams. Is all this healthy?

Tattoo on Hannah's ankle?

Feel numb.

Faith didn't bother to call in New York.

Noah nudged me and I looked up. Mr. Carlouci was staring at me. "Ms. Hansen, care to join us today?"

I mustered a polite smile. "I would love to." Which caused some snickering. I started scribbling notes in the journal, trying to look busy, which always makes teachers irrationally happy. After a bit of a stare-down, Mr. Carlouci started back up about the scientific method. But my mind was still connected to my father's, and it was a dark place.

The minute the bell sounded at three o'clock, I burst through the doors of the school with inhuman speed and went to the Rock. There I propped the journal up against a bump on the Rock's surface and scoured every page. I started back in March 2019 again.

Leave Faith?

Stay with Faith.

Feel stuck.

Leave.

Lied about promotion.

Haley won't talk to me.

Spends more time with Hannah. Too much time. So much anger.

Time for Hannah to get out of the picture?

Get out of the picture? It was all so sudden. What brings a man from being annoyed with his daughter's friend to wanting to get rid of her? I skimmed over the next few pages, too scared to read them in depth.

They got progressively worse and worse. The notes became more sporadic, and it seemed like he'd started taking them to remind himself of the lies he'd told so he could get his story straight. It detailed the increasingly large amount of alcohol he was consuming in private, the new car he'd bought and never used (or showed us), and how he had stopped showing up for work regularly, constantly claiming some sort of mild illness that was just bad enough to keep him out of work. While the contents of the pages were unpredictable, there was one constant: Hannah.

It seemed as though he was having an intense midlife crisis and Hannah and I were at the center of it. Why, exactly, I'm not sure. Maybe he thought getting rid of her would magically solve his problems.

I felt a nudge on my shoulder, and I jumped as I slammed the book shut. I looked to the left. It was just Rebecca. *Thank God.* I exhaled and relaxed.

"You okay there, Hale?" she asked with concern.

Hale. Don't call me Hale. Only Hannah can call me that.

"Um, yeah. I just found this." I passed the journal to Rebecca. There was no point hiding it from her.

Her expression was blank as she flipped through the pages. "Yep, this is pretty bad," she said. "Where'd you find it?"

I chewed at the fingernails on my good hand; the other was still a furious red. "I got questioned again this morning." Rebecca raised her eyebrows. I shook my head. "No, it wasn't that bad. They just wanted to ask me about Hannah and stuff. But come to think of it, it was kinda weird. They asked me if she reminded me of Allison."

"And did she?"

I shrugged. "I mean, a little." I paused to think about it for a second. "But it's not like they were the exact same person or anything."

Rebecca crossed her legs and rested her arms against a protruding bump on the Rock. She sighed. "What was she like?"

When I didn't answer, she said, "Hannah, I mean. What was she like?"

"She was special, like how you said Allison was. She was perfect, but she was flawed. Very. But there was something special about her. Like, you knew she had her problems, but you just kept coming back to her."

I know that wasn't a lot of words to describe her. Weird how hard it is to describe the most intense, complicated feelings you have and the people you feel them for. "But she was clueless. She never really knew the effect she had on people."

"Allison was like that too—clueless." Rebecca didn't look at me. "Well, not clueless. That sounds mean. Naive, I guess."

I scrunched up my face. "Naive? How so? No offense, Rebecca, but she seemed pretty socially aware."

"She was. But sometimes she couldn't even see what was happening right in front of her face." I didn't say anything. I wanted to ask more, but at the same time, I didn't want to pry too deeply. I knew it was a difficult time for her, and I didn't want to make everything hurt more than I already knew it did. But I didn't even need to ask, because Rebecca answered. "I loved her," she blurted out. Her deep brown eyes doubled in size like she couldn't believe she'd just told me that, like it was the first time she'd said it out loud.

"Loved her?" I was confused. Did Rebecca mean she loved Allison as a friend or as something more? If I remembered correctly, Allison was still dating Steven Liu when she died.

"Yeah." Rebecca's dark hair blew in the wind with the trees, blending in with the leaves and branches. "But she was so into Steven that she didn't even notice. It's not like she could've liked me back anyways." She sighed and closed her eyes as she tucked a rogue strand of hair behind her ear. "So I told her."

"Let me guess, the night before she was killed?"

Rebecca nodded. "Yeah. I just thought, you know, she was acting weird. Always on her phone. I thought that maybe she had been going through a rough patch with Steven and that maybe I had a shot or something." She let out a dry laugh. "Obviously I didn't. She was cool about it though, but it was still awkward, of course. She just told me that she couldn't feel the same way about me, and I told her I understood, and then we hugged and I left. That's the last time I saw her."

"So then if you didn't fight about that, what did you argue about?" God, I was starting to remind myself of Cook and Green. Too many questions too soon.

"I guess I was worried about our friendship. Sarah was just being a jerk, so I was mad about that—mad that Allison put up with it. I don't know. It was about nothing, really. Just a rant session, I guess." She laughed but then gulped, biting her lip to fight back the tears.

"Yeah," I said. I wasn't sure what else to say. We sat there, looking at the river, our hair blowing together in the wind. It was so strong, I almost fell over, knocking into her. We suddenly both laughed, and it felt like all our worries had just blown away too.

"You know what we should do?" Rebecca said. "Burn it."

"What?" I couldn't contain my bewilderment and at the same time curiosity. "Burn what?"

"The journal. I don't know." She smiled as her eyes danced. "You know how in *Friends*, Rachel, Phoebe, and Monica burn the stuff from their old boyfriends?" I nodded. "Okay, well, we should do that, but like for Allison and Hannah."

She hesitated for a moment, then grabbed my dad's journal from my hand and held it up like a torch. "To letting the past burn." We shared a smile. "Wait—burn it?" I asked. "Not to ruin the moment, but I've already got enough on my plate without an arson charge thrown into the mix."

"I wasn't being serious. I mean, we should destroy it, but I'm not really in the mood to get arrested either. You know what, let's just throw it in the river."

"Let's do it. What are you throwing in?"

She held up her finger as if to put me on pause.

Rebecca unzipped her backpack and shuffled around, looking for something. She finally pulled out a bracelet. "We got matching ones a few years back, Allison, Sarah, and I." She opened the journal and tucked the bracelet into one of the pockets inside the cover as I chewed my nail. *Does Rebecca really want to get rid of the bracelet?* It seemed like an odd choice to me. After Hannah died, I didn't dare throw away anything that she'd so much as looked at. But I guess everyone has different ways of dealing with grief. Rebecca had been a mess the last few days. Maybe she needed this. Still, I didn't want her to regret it later. She handed the journal to me. "Will you do the honors?"

I took it hesitantly, gazing out at the river, not sure why we were doing this but also trying to find a reason not to. What the heck, it seemed as good a time as any. There didn't seem any point in holding on to it.

Rebecca looked at me expectantly. Without another thought, I chucked the journal and bracelet into the current. We watched in silence as they drifted away. And I did feel a kind of release. On top of the Rock, wind in my face, I felt for a moment like all my troubles were drifting away.

"Thanks," said Rebecca after a while.

I scrunched up my nose. "Thanks? For what?" I was confused. If anything, Rebecca had given me a gift no one else had managed in the past few months: peace of mind.

"For helping me figure some stuff out. I'd invite you over or something, but I have some things I need to take care of first. Text you later, okay?"

"Yeah, sure." I smiled. Without Allison, I'd probably never have talked to Rebecca, and Jonas and I would probably each have continued pretending the other didn't exist. Rebecca hopped off the Rock, slung her backpack over her shoulder, and walked downstream in the direction we had thrown the journal and bracelet. "Catch you later," she yelled back at me before fading into the distance.

Then it crossed my mind. *What does Rebecca need to take care of? And why is she going through the woods and not back into town?*

I sat on the Rock for a while, unsure what to do with myself. I could go home and work on the murder board, but after my talk with Rebecca, I didn't feel like it. Perhaps she had given me hope—hope that I could be normal. I pulled out my phone to ask Jonas or Noah if they wanted to do anything, but a wave of tiredness washed over me like the river's current.

Maybe I could just go home, take a nap, and eat some ice cream. I could just do something for myself and by myself.

I jumped the fence and walked home. My mom was sitting at the kitchen table on the old family computer when I arrived. "Hey, honey," she said with a sweet smile. Either she had just screwed something up royally or she was genuinely excited to see me. You never know. Hopefully the latter.

She patted the stool next to her. "Here, take a seat." Her grin was still unbearably large. It was starting to make me uncomfortable.

"Well, you look happy. What's the occasion?" I asked as I slipped into the chair next to her.

She looked at me excitedly. Her eyes were bright, and her hair somehow looked less dull than it had the day before. "You'll never believe what happened today. I thought about what you said, and you're right. I need to move on, do something with my life. So …" She let the words hang in the air for a moment. "I got a job."

"Mom, that's so great," I shrieked. We both stood there in the kitchen, doing some sort of weird hug dance in our chairs. "So what is it?"

"Oh, not much. Just working a makeup counter at the Macy's a little ways away." I smiled. I wasn't surprised. Despite her weathered appearance, she was still a natural beauty with a knack for makeup. "It's not much, but it's something."

"Whatever, it still calls for a celebration."

My mother's eyes twinkled. She was clearly elated at the suggestion of some mother-daughter bonding that wasn't forced. "Sounds great," she said. "I'm thinking we order a pizza and work down some of that ice cream. I'll rent a movie. *The Princess Bride?*"

"Sure."

That night, I sat on the couch with my mother, my worries melting away like the ice cream we ate. I even almost forgot about the murder investigation and everything that went with it and whatever else the world wanted to throw at me.

Unfortunately, that feeling wouldn't last long.

16

The next morning, I was almost excited to go to school. *Almost.* Nothing could make compulsory education appealing.

Just like the previous morning, I rolled out of bed at 7:00, and just like the previous morning, Cook and Green were waiting for me in the kitchen. My mother wasn't around this time either.

I immediately sensed this meeting would be different than yesterday's before it even began. Cook and Green looked solemn. By comparison, they'd looked almost bored yesterday. "Why don't you take a seat?" said Cook, her voice devoid of all sarcasm and contempt. Strange.

I sat down and started shaking a bit as what felt like an unsettling cold breeze passed through the kitchen. I knit my fingers together to prevent myself from chewing on my nails. My eyes darted back and forth between the pair. Neither of them said anything. Part of me worried that they were there to arrest me.

When the silence became too much, I cleared my throat and asked the question uppermost in my mind. "So?"

This was enough to shake Cook from her trance, but Green still looked shaken up. "Erm." She glanced at Green but didn't receive any help from him. "Haley, were you friends with Rebecca Martinez?"

Were?

"Uh, yeah. I guess so. But only more recently. We just started hanging out in the past few days." Green's shoulders tensed up. Was he upset that I'd made a friend?

"Okay, well, then." Cook glanced at Green again. He remained emotionless. I was starting to question if this was the right career choice for him. While I wasn't the biggest fan of Cook, I couldn't deny that she was good at her job. "When was the last time you saw Ms. Martinez?"

"Why are you asking me this? Is Rebecca okay?"

"Ms. Hansen," piped up Cook, "that is beside the point. Now answer the question. When was the last time you saw Rebecca Martinez?"

I folded my arms tightly. I didn't want to answer their questions until they told me what had happened to Rebecca, but they both looked so serious that I didn't want to question their judgment. I settled on "Yesterday after school."

Green pulled out his notepad and started to write everything down.

"At approximately what time would you say you were together and where?"

"Probably at 3:30, for about an hour or so. Maybe a little less. We were just on this large rock next to the river across from the school."

"And you were together the whole time? No one else joined you?" she asked. Green stared me dead in the eyes while he continued to scribble furiously on his pad.

"Um, yeah," I said. I didn't mean to sound so uncertain, but Green's writing was starting to distract me. A sound that would otherwise be comforting felt like nails on a chalkboard.

"What happened after that? Where did you go and where did she go?"

My eyes darted between the pair. Their gaze was unwavering. It was suffocating.

"I stayed at the Rock for a little while, and Rebecca went downstream." They looked at me expectantly. Maybe that wasn't good enough for them. "Then I went home and was with my mom for the rest of the night."

"Can anyone verify this?" asked Cook in an accusatory tone.

"My mom can. That I was with her all night, I mean. My Life 360 could, but apparently you guys don't really roll with that." I had meant it as a joke, but neither of them changed their expression. If anything, Cook's glare got a bit more intense.

"And what was Rebecca like when she left you? Was she acting weird, or did she say anything that stood out to you?" Green was asking the questions now. He passed the notepad and pen to Cook.

This caught me off guard, because she had. "Yes," I told them. Cook started writing. "Before she left, she said that she wanted to hang out longer but she 'had something to take care of.' Then she walked downstream, which struck me as odd because we always head back towards the school after going to the Rock. You know, to get back to the sidewalk. I'm not even sure what's in that direction." They looked at each other. "Why are you asking me this, anyways? Is Rebecca okay? When you asked if I *were* friends with Rebecca, what were you trying to imply?"

Cook stopped writing and looked at Green, who leaned forward.

He sighed. "Ms. Hansen, we didn't want to be the ones to have to tell you this, but you'll find out eventually." *Ms. Hansen, not Haley.* "This morning, Rebecca was found dead in the woods near where you last saw her." I started sobbing. "And we're currently investigating it as a homicide," he added.

When you're faced with something that you can't handle, it's an out-of-body experience, like you suddenly become a spectator watching yourself go to pieces. That was what I was experiencing, and not for the first time. A deep, pained wail escaped my throat, mixing with my sobbing. Cook and Green looked at each other. Finally, Green spoke, taking a more authoritative tone. "We need to speak with your mother immediately to make sure you were here last night. We're sorry we couldn't wait until she came home this morning, but we have two girls dead in less than a week. We have no time to wait at this point."

I gave a noncommittal shrug. The sadness suddenly subsided, replaced by a jolt of anger. I bolted straight to my bedroom. Cook and Green stood up, pushing their chairs aside.

All I knew was that Hannah was dead. And Allison. And Rebecca. And that it was probably somehow my fault, and I didn't know why.

I kicked the door of my room open and ran to the Post-it-covered wall. One by one, I tore them all down, screaming as I did so. I threw them on the carpet and smashed them with my feet like they were skittering cockroaches. I sunk down on the floor. I was a mess. My mom suddenly came bursting through the door and knelt down to take me in a bear hug.

"Oh, baby," she said, rocking me back and forth. "I'm here, I'm here." I turned around and looked at her through the haze of tears. After a few minutes—or a few hours; at this point I was too dazed to know—she walked out of the room and had a muffled conversation with Cook and Green, who must have been standing in the hallway the whole time. Soon I heard the front door open and close. They were gone.

She lifted my rag doll body onto my bed and stroked my hair. "I'll make you a hot chocolate. Why don't you try and get some sleep?"

Her footsteps grew quiet as she went off to the kitchen. I could still hear her moving around. After a few minutes, I heard the ring of the landline. *Odd. No one ever uses that anymore.* Then I closed my eyes and shuffled in my bed, trying to get comfortable. My mother was right; I needed some shut-eye to try to take my mind off Rebecca. Despite having slept a sufficient amount the night before, I was completely drained.

I tried to let sleep take me, but I couldn't. It was like my brain simply would not turn off. All I could think about was the last thing Rebecca had said, that she had "something to take care of." It didn't make sense. We had completely opened up to each other, and then suddenly she went all mysterious on me. Why didn't she just tell me what she was doing? Why hadn't I asked?

My thoughts were interrupted by my mother's slow and steady voice as she talked to the person on the telephone. This told me it wasn't a telemarketer as I had thought. We had a policy in our house that as soon as we received a call from a tabloid or someone trying to buy our story, we immediately disconnected the phone. I tuned in my ears to listen to the conversation.

"Yes, I understand." She paused.

A low mumble was audible from the kitchen. I slowly left the covers and crept up to the wall to hear her better. I placed my left ear against the wall and listened. "She's not up to it right now." Anger crept into her voice. My mother could be many things—sarcastic, numb, and depressed—but angry was rarely one of them. The voice remained steady on the other line. "I said she's not ready. My daughter is not a criminal." My blood ran cold. The static of the telephone was the only thing audible for about a minute or so; my mother said nothing. "Fine," she said. She hung up the phone and her footsteps grew closer.

I gasped. I was never going to make it back to bed in time. My mother opened the door silently with the hot chocolate in hand. I stood there in the middle of the room, not saying anything. She cocked her head to the side. "Haley, what are you doing up?"

"Who was that?" I asked forcefully. My brain was jumbled, but one thing was clear: I needed to know who she was talking to. Especially if it was about me.

She sighed and placed the hot chocolate down on the desk. "I didn't want to overwhelm you." She crossed her arms sternly.

"But ..." I trailed off, hoping she would finish the sentence.

"That was Detective Green. They need to bring you in for questioning again."

I groaned and plopped back onto the bed.

"Why? What did I do wrong?" I stared at the ceiling, thinking about how unfair everything was, hating the world and the losing hand it had dealt me.

My mother sat down on the edge of my bed and crossed her legs. She scrunched up her face like she wasn't really sure what to say. "They found something with your friend."

I didn't look at her; I just shifted onto my side and stared at the wall. My life was a horror movie, and someone else was writing the script. She cleared her throat. "But that's beside the point. I don't think they think you're a suspect."

"Why do you say that?"

"The thing is, they said whatever they found doesn't link you to the murder, but it could help link it to someone else."

"Well, what was it?" She was making no sense to me. Why keep talking about this "something" but not tell me what it was?

"They said they want to wait until tomorrow."

-

School was canceled that day and Friday, so I had plenty of time to mull it over. I considered calling Noah or Jonas, but I wasn't quite sure what to say. This was different from Allison's death. Rebecca we actually knew—and liked. I couldn't imagine what Noah was going through right now. Well, actually, I could.

So I did nothing but lie in bed until I eventually fell asleep. The next morning, I slipped on a pair of leggings and a sweatshirt and drove with my mom down to the police station.

The police station was surprisingly cold-hearted for a small town. Fort Vepar, for all its faults, had a cute downtown full of antique shops and old brownstone stores; there was a real Mayberry Main Street vibe to it all. But the police station looked transported from Soviet Russia—a box of gray concrete that seemed to absorb the sunlight and convert it into dread. We walked in and were greeted by a desk sergeant who matched the décor perfectly. She was pale with slicked-back hair, a long, downturned nose, thick glasses, and a permanent scowl, which she used on me with great effect while we took a seat in the lobby.

Finally, Green opened a door and ushered me into a small room. It must have been where they questioned people. The walls were gray and the floor had tan tiles. There was one window and a lighting fixture, flickering subtly, that hung over a metal desk and matching chairs.

Green motioned for me to sit down in one of the chairs, and he took a seat in the one across from me. Next, he took the familiar metal tape recorder out of his pocket and placed it in the middle of the table.

17

Interview with Haley Hansen, November 15, 2019, 1:03 p.m.

Detective Green: Good afternoon, Ms. Hansen.

Haley Hansen: Likewise.

DG: Do you have any idea why you're here?

HH: My mom mentioned that something was left with Rebecca. (pause) She also said that I'm not being questioned as a suspect anymore, correct?

DG: I'm afraid that I can neither confirm nor deny this. But what I can say is that you are here today so that we can make an inquiry about an object. Understood?

HH: Yes, but I still don't know what it is. Can I see it?

(Suspect is shown the piece of evidence.

Evidence Description:

Evidence in question is a framed photograph. Four by six inches. Photograph depicts Haley Hansen and Hannah Schulz. Date the photograph was taken is unknown. HS has X's through eyes and HH is untouched.)

DG: Is this yours?

HH: Yes. (pause) It's usually on my desk. I noticed that it was gone last Wednesday, but I didn't think much of it.

DG: When during the day did you first notice it was missing?

HH: That morning, right after you and Cook, sorry, Detective Cook, visited me.

DG: So the photograph could have gone missing on an earlier date?

HH: Yeah, yes. But I remember it still being there Tuesday morning.

(Audible writing)

DG: So the picture could have gone missing any time after Tuesday morning to Wednesday morning?

HH: Correct.

DG: Was there anyone besides you and your mother in the house during the aforementioned time frame?

HH: Yes. I had a few friends over Tuesday afternoon and then you and Detective Cook were there Wednesday morning before I woke up.

DG: Who were these friends?

HH: Rebecca. And then two other people. Noah and Jonas.

DG: Are Jonas and Noah also students at Fort Vepar High School?

HH: Yeah. They're both juniors too.

DG: And these were the only people inside the house besides you and your mother?

HH: Yes. Well, you'd have to ask my mother, but I doubt she had anyone over. And you and Detective Cook.

DG: Are you certain that the photograph went missing and that you are not the one who left it at the crime scene?

HH: I'm certain. I think I'd remember doing that.

DG: Okay then. (pause) Do you think that any of your friends could have taken the portrait?

HH: No. Maybe Rebecca did and her killer found it on her, I'm not sure. Just an idea.

DG: A very specific idea. Last question: can you think of anyone who would have wanted to harm Rebecca?

HH: No—well, yes. Not necessarily harm her, per se. Rebecca and Sarah stopped talking to each other after Allison died. Rebecca mentioned that they weren't friends anymore, which I found odd, but not really.

DG: What do you mean by that?

HH: I don't know Sarah well. Not at all, actually. But I did over-hear her and Rebecca arguing the day of the memorial. While I was in the bathroom. It just seemed like their overall friendship was kind of toxic for all parties involved.

DG: Do you know what they argued about that day?

HH: I'm not sure, completely. I only overheard the end of their conversation. But from what I could tell, Rebecca felt that Sarah was using Allison.

DG: Using her?

HH: Yeah, like for her popularity and stuff. Rebecca said that Sarah didn't actually like Allison for Allison, just liked the perks that came with it. The parties, the boys. You know.

DG: Do you think Sarah was angry enough to harm Rebecca (pause) or have a motive for killing Allison?

HH: As I've said before, I don't know Sarah, and I didn't know Allison. But no … maybe. I don't know.

Interview terminated at 1:15 p.m.

18

If I've learned one thing in my life, it's that people aren't shades of black and white. We're all just kind of floating around in this gray area, pretending that we're good. But we all have secrets. We all have sinned.

Take my father, for example. He was a clean-cut guy; he never raised his voice. He seemed like a pretty okay person. He was a loving father and husband. He took a job he didn't really like in a town he didn't really like so he could give me a good upbringing in a safe place. He had friends, hosted neighborhood barbecues on the Fourth of July.

Yet at the same time, he had a dark side that he kept hidden from us all. He was jealous, calculating. Obsessive too. He was even a murderer.

Sometimes I worry that I'm like that too. I have weird dreams where I'm in his mind, feeling that murderous rage and doing the terrible things he did. But they're just dreams. Like everyone, I put a mask on every day and hide my secrets from the world. But in truth, everyone is like that to some extent.

Hannah was, and Rebecca too. Maybe even Allison.

Hannah tried to glide easily through life like nothing in the world could harm her. But it could. And did.

Rebecca was the same way. From afar, her mask seemed impenetrable, like she was unbothered by the world. She wasn't closed off, exactly, not like Hannah was. She was untouchable.

But she was soft inside too. She loved Allison and she loved her friends. She was almost too vulnerable to her emotions.

Sometimes I think *Is everyone like this? Or are some people just as cold as they seem?* Come to think of it, I had never seen Sarah's emotions crack. She never once showed remorse or vulnerability. So was she capable of murdering Allison and Rebecca in cold blood? Only time could tell, but I didn't have it.

19

Green held the door open for me as I exited the police station. "We'll keep in touch," he told me before I left. My mom was waiting for me by the curb in the car. I slid into the passenger seat and buckled up my seat belt. My mom looked at me suspiciously with her hands on the steering wheel, staring me up and down. After a moment or two, she snapped out of it.

"So?" She looked at me expectantly. "How'd it go?"

I shrugged. "Fine, I guess. They just needed to talk to me because a picture of me and Hannah was found next to Rebecca."

She gasped. "How'd it get there? You didn't lend it to anyone, did you? Or did someone break in?" Her eyes were so large they were almost cartoonish. If she hadn't been genuinely scared, I might have found it funny, even.

"No, I didn't lend it to anyone. Why would someone want to borrow a picture of my dead friend? Try not to worry too much, Mom. You didn't hear anyone in the house, right? Because I didn't hear anyone, and the picture was next to my bed. I'm not sure what happened, though. The best theory I've got is that Rebecca might have swiped it when she was over at the house a few days ago and the killer found it on her."

She nodded and her eyes shrunk back down to their normal size, but she still looked shaken. I thought that maybe she was worried that if someone had broken in and seen the portrait then they knew who we were. She closed her eyes and took a deep breath, then rolled away from the curb and towards the house.

I looked out the window. Out of the corner of my eye, I could see Cook staring at me from the back of the police station.

We were silent almost all the way home. We had just pulled up to the driveway when my phone buzzed in my pocket. It was Jonas.

Jonas: question 6, will you meet me at the rock?

Haley: OMW.

"Mom?" I asked. She grunted softly to let me know she was listening, half concentrated on the road and half concentrated on me. "Can you drop me off right here?"

She looked flustered. "Why?"

"Just meeting a friend near school."

My mother sighed. "Sweetie, are you sure this is a good idea? I mean, two murders in a week. I'm not sure if it's safe." She looked sad and confused, but she was right, and not in a good way. We're never certain that anything is a good idea, but we do things anyway. My mom thought marrying my dad was a good idea, and look how that turned out.

"Don't worry, I trust him and we'll be out in public the whole time." That was not entirely accurate, I guess, though technically we would be on public land.

She slowed the car to a stop and I climbed out, giving her a kiss and a quick "I love you" before walking to the school.

A few steps down the road, my mother put the car in reverse and pulled up next to me. "Be careful, Haley," she yelled before driving off towards the house. I flashed her a thumbs-up and continued on my way. It was only a few minutes' walk. I found Jonas waiting for me right where I expected.

He looked ... different. On edge, I guess. He looked deathly pale with deep bags under his eyes. His hoodie and jeans were black, as usual, but today they made him look like the Grim Reaper. It was a somber look that pretty much matched the mood of Fort Vepar.

"Hey," I said. He gave me a weak smile in reply. I climbed the Rock and sat next to him. If you looked closely enough and squinted your eyes, you could see the police tape in the distance where Rebecca had gone.

"How are you holding up?" Jonas asked. I shrugged. "I get that," he said. "I can't believe it either. It was just a few days ago that we were with her. It's just hard to believe, you know?"

"Yeah, and I feel like we were just getting to know her too. I feel like I've just wasted so much time."

"Me too," he said. "Care to go for a walk?"

"Sure." I hopped off the Rock and almost landed in the river, letting out a small shriek. Jonas rolled his eyes at me.

"Might as well cross," he said. After a moment, he jumped into the river, splashing water all over me. I let out a surprised gasp and looked at him. His hands flew to his mouth, like he regretted splashing me.

I couldn't help but laugh, though I was kind of pissed. The look on his face was so ridiculous. He dropped his hands and laughed too. He reached out to me and I took his hand hesitantly. He pulled me into the water, making me laugh harder.

Together, we crossed to the other side and started walking in the same direction that Rebecca had gone. There was no police tape on this side of the stream.

"Have the cops spoken to you yet?" I asked him. While this may have seemed like an enigmatic question, it felt completely justified. They'd been bugging practically everyone since the murders, and Jonas was in the frame as a friend of Rebecca.

Jonas shook his head. "No. I still don't understand why they keep questioning you, though. How many times has it been now? Two? Three?"

"Four," I said dryly. Guilt tugged at my heartstrings. I wanted to tell Jonas about Hannah and my dad and everything. It felt like I was living a lie, even being an accomplice to the murderer themselves. I reminded myself that I hadn't told any lies, exactly. More like half-truths and just maybe some lies of omission, but I was trying to keep my head above water.

Jonas lifted his eyebrows so high that I swear they almost went right into his hairline. "What? Isn't that, like, illegal or something? I mean, questioning without sufficient evidence."

"I'm not sure. Probably," I replied solemnly. "We can't afford a lawyer, and my mom and I aren't really up to speed on criminal law."

Jonas stopped walking beside me. "Then why haven't you said anything?" He looked concerned and genuinely confused. I suddenly stopped walking. I couldn't do this anymore.

"Because"—I took a deep breath—"they do have evidence against me. A decent amount, actually." Jonas bit his lip and looked down, speechless. That was when I knew it was the wrong thing to tell him. *There goes my last friend.*

It would be too painful to lose him too. After Hannah and Rebecca, I just couldn't take it. Especially now that Noah was barely speaking to me. "I didn't do it. Please, Jonas, you have to believe me—"

"I do." He cut me short. He looked me in the eyes with a steady gaze. "I just ... I just don't understand." He looked hurt, which hurt me. If I hadn't already felt guilty enough about everything that had happened, I certainly did now. "I just don't get it, Haley. I'm trying, but I just don't. Do you not trust me?" He looked like a sad puppy.

"I'm sorry. I do trust you. I just can't explain right now." I gulped. The last thing I wanted to do right now was cry.

"I'm sorry too, Haley, because I'm gonna need you to." He paused. "Please understand."

I exhaled deeply. "Okay. Just promise to believe me. And not to tell *anyone.* Not even Noah."

"I promise," he told me.

I started walking slowly down the side of the stream. *Keep walking.* "I'm sorry I haven't told you guys everything. Because

I honestly don't know what to tell people. Everything's still so raw for me." He looked into my eyes, hanging onto my every word. *Here goes.* "Do you know who Dan Hansen is?"

"Yeah. Well, no." He nodded. "That's the guy you told us about when we went to your house. But you said he's not related to you." Understanding slowly dawned on his face. "But that's not true?"

A bitter taste settled at the back of my mouth. "I lied. I'm sorry." To my surprise, he didn't look mad or upset that I hadn't told him. He just nodded at me and we kept walking.

"And the girl he killed, she was my best friend for literally forever. That's why we moved here—too many ghosts in our old town. And everyone thought it was my fault, even if they wouldn't say it out loud. They all thought I was some type of devil spawn or something. Everywhere I went was a constant reminder of what happened, which is why my mom and I don't tell anyone. Please understand." He didn't say anything. "Please say something, anything. Tell me I'm a bad friend or whatever. I don't care. Anything."

"I'm sorry," he said finally.

I shook my head. "No, don't be sorry. You have nothing to be sorry for."

"It's just not fair," he replied. "That bad things happen to good people."

I sighed a breath of relief. He wasn't mad at me, and he didn't think I'd done it, either. This was such a best-case scenario that I hadn't even considered it in the realm of possibilities.

"Well, if they actually have something against you, we really have to solve it now."

"Like we weren't trying before?" I had to hold down confused laughter. This wasn't the moment for that.

"I mean, yeah, because that's what you wanted." He paused. "But I guess I wasn't taking it all that seriously before. At least, not as seriously as I should have been." He trudged forward and looked down at his sneakers instead of at me.

"And why's that?" I asked, genuinely wanting to know.

He shrugged. "This is going to sound terrible, but I didn't really know Allison or Rebecca. Yeah, I knew them from school, but it didn't feel like anything really happened to me, if you know what I mean. And us trying to solve the murder, it felt a bit like we were in a *Scooby-Doo* episode. I don't know anything about solving a murder." Then Jonas stopped in his tracks. "I've never gone this far," he said.

"Neither have I," I confessed. "Keep walking to the end?" He nodded. I had always assumed that the river ran for at least a few more miles in this direction, since it was so short in the other. It turned out that it flowed under a bridge through a big, rusty culvert. It was basically a tunnel covered with a metal grating made up of squares that let the water flow through. There was very little debris on the grate—the stream ran mostly through gravel and flowed freely.

When we made it to the end, Jonas said, "I'll bet you ten bucks I can climb this thing." I laughed, but then something on the grating caught my attention.

"Wait. Hold on," I said forcefully. Slowly but steadily, I walked into the stream once again to take a closer look. Something was caught on the grating, being beaten around by the rapid current. Once I was a few feet away, it was clear what it was. Blue, green, pink, and purple strings woven into an intricate pattern. Rebecca's bracelet.

This alone wasn't particularly troubling. If anything, I was happy to be able to hold on to some part of her, no matter how small. What was disturbing was not the presence of the bracelet but the absence of something else. The book.

While it was a miracle that the bracelet had gotten stuck on the grating, it was impossible that the book hadn't. There was no way it could have drifted past. The squares were too small, about a quarter of its size. There was nowhere for it to go unless someone had taken it.

"Hey, Jonas?" I called out. He looked up at me expectantly. "I should probably start heading home. My mom wants me to get back soon, you know, just to make sure that I'm safe and stuff." Another half-truth. It burned at the back of my throat.

"Yeah, sure," he said nonchalantly. He had surprised me today in a good way. I had only really known him for a week, but I already felt so comfortable with him. I felt like I could tell him anything—things that I might not have even told Hannah. I quickly pocketed the bracelet and waved goodbye to Jonas. I broke into a slow jog along the bank and crossed the stream where the police tape ended.

I hadn't considered how suspicious walking near the river might look, so I decided that I might as well look for Cook or Green so I could tell them about the journal. While this thought crossed my mind, I couldn't bring myself to actually execute it. It was like there was a beehive in my brain, but I guess they couldn't make honey, just like I couldn't make coherent thoughts.

I trudged home quickly, soaked up to my knees in river water. I probably looked a little crazy. Heck, if I wasn't me, I might have thought that I was the killer.

I fumbled with the lock on my front door and bolted into my room, giving my mother a hurried hello. I fell to my knees and crawled around in the pile of torn Post-it notes and looked for the slip of paper with the phone number Green had given me. But that too had gone missing.

20

Since I had basically destroyed anything and everything in sight during my rage, I was back at ground zero. I needed to start afresh. I pulled every box out of my closet and threw the small number of clothes I owned onto the floor close by. Soon the wall of the closet was bare and I had a clean slate to work with. My mother poked her head through the door one or two times, looking more confused than concerned.

I fumbled through the boxes and began writing on the backs of old letters and unused stationery. I found an old box of thumbtacks that, at the expense of my wall, made it much easier to visualize things. On two of the largest folders, I scribbled Rebecca and Allison's names and placed them on opposite sides of the closet. Everything that I knew about either of them was in between. I tried repeatedly to find some type of link between what had happened to both of them, but it was so ... messy. The only thing that was clear about Allison and Rebecca's murders was Hannah and, by default, my dad.

Then it occurred to me that after the first week of the murder, I had completely stopped checking up on the case on the internet. *Why would I?* Last time I checked, my dad was a murderer and psychopath.

It had never once occurred to me that there was more to the story than I knew. I had always just assumed that being "involved" in the crime firsthand meant that I knew more about it than anyone else because I knew the people. But I hadn't been there for everything.

It was too painful to read about the trial and see what people on the internet were saying about Hannah and my father, and therefore me—even if they didn't know who I was. It was a scary thought.

But sometimes we need to do the things that scare us to make them less terrifying, to ground them in reality. What was the worst thing that could happen? Becoming informed about something that actually pertained to me? *Yes.* But sometimes ignorant bliss is more painful than the truth—or maybe not. I just didn't know how much longer I could go without knowing.

I creaked the door open and checked the time on the microwave. 11 p.m. My mother would surely be asleep by now. Nevertheless, I tried not to breathe as I tiptoed over to the kitchen counter to get the family laptop.

My mother might not like me snooping around, per se, even if it was *my* business. I didn't want to look up stuff on my school computer; they'd probably think I was a creep and gladly hand over any info on it to the cops. My best option was to take the laptop, clear the history, and put it back before my mother noticed. I returned to my room and jumped onto my bed, sitting criss-cross applesauce with the computer on my lap.

The bright glow of the screen burned my eyes. *Dan Hansen,* I typed into the search bar. I scrolled down, trying to soak up as much information as I could before I had to put it back.

The first page of links mostly led me to news articles about the trial. I began with those but found nothing unexpected. Full confession, strong forensic evidence, you know the drill. The only thing that stood out about the trial in any way was that my dad had defended his actions, stood by them. He claimed that he'd done it for me to protect me from being corrupted.

Moving on. I continued to scroll down the pages of search results. I pretty much considered everything past the first two pages as the dark web. Perfect.

The second page led me to more news articles from lesser-known sites and a couple of blog posts. Not much different from the first page but definitely less credible. On the third page, the credible new articles almost completely disappeared, replaced by opinion articles with my father's mugshot on the front and a good deal of clickbait.

The fourth page was where things truly got weird. It linked me to pieces such as "10 Reasons Why Dan Hansen's Actions Were Justified" and "Take This Short Quiz to Find Out How Similar You Are to Dan Hansen."

Reassuringly for humanity, the comment sections were flooded with general disgust and calls to take them down.

By now it was 1 a.m. I had scoured every article on the first four pages and was just starting on the fifth page. At first sight, it looked very similar to the fourth page, but at the bottom, the narrative seemed to shift. It started with articles like "Dan Hansen Gives Voice to Today's Teens." How ironic, because he took Hannah's away. But I could always pass these off as the ramblings of a screwed-up mind.

But I kept going further down the rabbit hole. There was fanfiction, of all things, and theories about what happened in Hannah's last moments. My breathing started to get heavier as a sense of dread took hold. Soon it was hard to breathe and easy to believe that I was having a heart attack, but the logical slice of my brain reassured me that was impossible. I was a reasonably healthy sixteen-year-old.

I tried the breathing exercises I had learned in counseling after Hannah's death but found my efforts futile. I checked the time on my phone. Two o'clock. I clicked off the search results and tried looking through some happy things, like a slideshow of the world's cutest puppies. But it didn't really help, so I resolved to dive back into the filth and get through this. I knew I had to get through this.

I clicked back to my search and forced myself to read. Of course, I didn't read the fanfiction. That would tip me too far over the edge.

But I did skim what people were saying. There was a lot of praise for one "creator" in particular. Links from his profile took me to a Reddit page with a discussion about my dad. It was pretty heated, but most people chiming into the discussion were pro-Hansen.

For some reason, this didn't surprise me.

The username was jbgHansen_ug5m03i4. It was not exactly the most easily decipherable username I'd ever come across. It sounded like someone had slammed the keyboard, written my last name, and slammed the keyboard again. What happened to just using your favorite movie character or something? *Probably not wanting to get caught.* I had to admit, there was something oddly liberating about being able to be someone else, even for just a little while. But in this case, it wouldn't help me get anywhere. I continued stalking the account.

jbgHansen_ug5m03i4 wrote about Dan Hansen quite often, according to his or her profile. The most recent post was from the previous day. It read:

All we hear about is the pain that Hannah suffered, but what about the pain Dan Hansen suffered? What about his daughter and the millions of people just like her? Are we just going to stand by and watch as people like Hannah Schulz can get away with tormenting people because "no one got hurt"? I'm sick of it, and I bet that you are too. Dan Hansen just did what we're too chicken to do. So let me ask you this; why is standing up against this a bad thing? #supportdanhansen

I tried to hold back the hot bile in my throat, but it was a losing effort. I ran to the hallway bathroom and let it all just spill out of me. I lay there on the floor, curled into a ball, trying to process everything. #supportdanhansen—was that some type of cruel joke from someone with a very twisted sense of humor? God, I hoped so. My stomach rumbled again. From the puking or hunger, I couldn't tell. Probably both. I lifted myself off the cold bathroom tiles and decided to go into the kitchen for a glass of water.

"What the hell is this, Haley?" Mom yelled, pointing at the screen of the laptop, sitting silently on my bed. "What are you doing?"

"I was just doing some digging about Dad and I found that." I pointed to the jbgHansen_ug5m03i4 post. "I didn't write it!"

My mother shook her head. "I can't believe this. I've spent all this time running away from what happened, and now you want to bring it right back into our lives!"

"I'm looking because I know nothing," I shot back. "I haven't heard from or about him since before the trial. He's my dad. I have to know. I just thought ... Dad had a reason, right?"

She looked bewildered. "No!"

"No, stop it. Let me finish," I said. "I'm just trying to understand why someone would kill Allison and Rebecca." I choked their names out. "Maybe if I could see how these people think, I could understand. The murders, they're all connected to Hannah and Dad somehow. And me. I need to understand, to find a motive. It might help me catch Allison and Rebecca's—"

"Woah, whoa, whoa. Slow down." My mom let out a slight groan. I had forgotten how late it was. "Don't get involved in this. You'll just make it worse. This isn't your business, it's the detectives'."

"No, Mom. It is my business. Someone stole my picture of Hannah. It might have been Rebecca, but still. Someone knows about us besides Cook and Green. If I just sit back and let this happen, I'll never be able to live with myself!"

Without warning, she slammed the screen of the laptop down against the keyboard. I jumped. "I better not catch you looking at this stuff again. Stay out of it. Believe it or not, people are working very hard to make sure nothing bad happens to us." And with that, she drifted down the hallway back to her room, laptop in hand.

21

It was a week after Hannah's death and I still hadn't been able to find any closure. None at all. After Hannah's funeral, we'd decided to move, but there was something I had to do first. The only thing that I thought could make me make sense of it all: visiting my dad.

I didn't want to see him because he was my father; he wasn't anymore. Now he was just that man who killed Hannah. I needed to ask him why. *Why Hannah? What did she ever do to him? And, selfishly, how could he do this to me?* There was no reasonable explanation.

My mom had made countless phone calls to him throughout the week but hadn't actually visited yet.

The prison was gray and cold. We went through multiple checkpoints, each one more humiliating than the last, waiting at each one as they checked our names, checked my mom's purse, took our cell phones, and patted us down to make sure we weren't planning on passing anything on to my dad. We went through brightly lit, white hallways filled with the constant buzz of metal doors being clanked open and shut. Every step of the way, I felt eyes on me, and the farther in we went, the stronger the feeling that they weren't going to let us back out.

We finally got to the visitation room, a small box with off-white walls that made it feel a little warmer than the hallways. It was still filled with that sense of dread. My dad sat at a gray metal table, his hands cuffed in front of him to a metal loop on the table. An overweight guard stood at the back of the room, not saying a word but watching us with unsympathetic eyes.

My dad. He looked over at us with a smug, sickening little grin. He looked satisfied with himself, like us being here together was some kind of victory. I suddenly had the urge to ask my mom if we could turn around and go home, pack our things and leave today.

But I didn't. I sat down on an uncomfortable, sharp-edged chair across the wide table from my dad. I stared at him for a moment, speechless. I wanted him to know just how much I despised him. "Hello, Haley," he said with a smile. I didn't return it.

He looked no different than he had a week ago. It was clear that he felt no remorse for what he had done, and I needed to know why. I just stared him down for a few moments, trying my best not to change my expression. But I couldn't hold my cool and calm exterior for long, and soon I was sobbing. I covered my eyes with my hands for a moment, trying to collect my thoughts. Finally, I looked across the table at him. "Can you tell me why you did it?"

"Now, sweetie, that's no way to talk to your dear old dad."

"Don't call me that," I shouted.

That threw him off a bit. He shuffled uncomfortably on his stool on the other side of the glass. "Haley, like it or not, I am your father." I glared at him. My mother hovered in the corner of the room, speechless. For all of her phone calls and efforts to get him out of prison, she didn't seem too warm toward him. It was like she wanted the idea of being a family back, not him. "That's why I did it, you know."

I shook my head. "What's 'why'?"

He laughed snarkily like he knew something I didn't and that made him so much smarter than me. "You know why, Haley. You won't understand now, but you'll understand later."

"I don't understand! Hannah is ... was my best friend, you know that!"

He sighed. "No, she wasn't."

"Is that why you did it? Is that why you killed her? Were you jealous or something?"

He tapped the counter in front of him and leaned back in his chair. "So you really want to know why I did it, then." His eyes wandered down to his feet. My dad seemed disappointed, like he wanted me to ask him how it felt or congratulate him or something sick like that.

"Yes. Why else would I be asking?"

He huffed. "Fine. Maybe then you could bring yourself to forgive me."

"I doubt that."

"We'll see." Dan Hansen rested his forearms on the table in front of him and leaned forward. "I did it for you, Haley. Can't you see that?"

I scoffed. "What do you mean, you did it for me? I didn't want Hannah dead."

"I know it's not what you wanted, but it's what you needed. You should be thankful. I hope someday when you're older and your headaches stop and you can think clearly, you'll appreciate what I've done," he said. "But part of me hopes that day never comes. Either way, I want you to know this—everything I've done, I've done for you, and I would gladly do it again."

And that was that. There was no use trying to convince my dad what he'd done was wrong. It was like trying to convince a toddler that their imaginary friend wasn't real; it just wouldn't work.

There was nothing left for me here. Nothing that could give me closure. It was time to leave. I glanced at my mom and she nodded. I stood up and pushed my chair back under the counter, then took one last look at my father, because I knew this would be the last time I would ever see him.

Going into the visit, I'd thought that my father might be sorry. And maybe I'd thought that if he was, I might be able to forgive him. Or at least try to. But I was wrong, and so was my father. I'd never forgive him, because not even time heals some wounds.

22

And then it was the weekend. *Great.* It was hard to believe that it was just last week that Allison was murdered. It felt like a lifetime ago.

When I woke up and went to the kitchen for breakfast, the family laptop wasn't in its usual spot. When my mom wandered in and I asked her about it, she just said, "Don't test me, Haley." From the tone of her voice, I knew that testing her was the last thing I'd want to do. She was already dressed and ready to go to her new job. She had to pick up extra shifts over the weekend to make up for taking care of me for the past few days.

The moment after she walked out the front door and rolled the car down the driveway, I scoured the house but couldn't find the laptop anywhere. I went back to my room and grabbed my phone to call in the cavalry.

Haley: Do you have a laptop?

Jonas: no, why??

It's important.

Noah has one.

Do you think he's up for a meet and greet right now?

are you?

No, but it's important. Now I said it twice!! Tell Noah that.

on it.

When he didn't text back for a few minutes, I took that as a no from Noah. But sure enough, my phone buzzed in my pocket with a reply from Jonas.

meet at the cool beans in 20?

Be there, I typed quickly with flying thumbs. The Cool Beans was a small coffee shop on the far side of town, and the only one with free Wi-Fi. Apparently, Fort Vepar was not deemed important enough for a Starbucks. We usually stayed away from it, because it was a popular spot among Sarah's crowd and packed to the brim. And expensive. And it was one of those smart places that prided itself on having organic, free-range, pesticide-free, fair-trade, hand-washed, solar-roasted beans. On top of all that, it was two miles away.

Nevertheless, it would have to do. By the time I got to the Cool Beans, Jonas and Noah were already there. They were huddled in a small cushy booth in the corner. The place had bean bags mixed with booths. The lights were dimmed, and smooth, slow jazz was playing on the sound system.

Noah was hunched over the laptop, the light from the screen giving his face a bluish tint. Jonas, on the other hand, was leaning back against the booth, hugging a cushion tight in his lap. *Cute.*

"What's up?" I asked as I slid into the booth, made out of wood so old and lacquered it could have come from a 1920s speakeasy.

"Hey," said Jonas. Noah gave me a noncommittal grunt. "That's what we were going to ask you," said Jonas after a minute.

"Well, I'm sitting here, ready to get cracking. How are you doing, Noah?" I asked. He shrugged without bothering to look up from the laptop. I couldn't tell if he was still not really talking to me or if he was so upset that he wasn't able to speak anymore.

"Noah's not really in the mood for talking," Jonas confirmed. I put my hand on Noah's shoulder to try to comfort him instead. He didn't shrug me off, but I could feel his shoulders tense up.

Jonas pushed a pitcher and a teapot towards me slowly. "Would you like the complimentary water or the green tea that we were required to buy so they wouldn't kick us out?"

"Complimentary water, please," I said. "So, I need to look at a few things on the laptop." Noah closed his tabs and slid the laptop over so it was facing me.

Jonas stole a glance over my shoulder. "Like what?" he asked.

I twisted the screen so that he could see it clearly. "I found this, like, series of accounts online about Dan Hansen. My mom took the laptop away, and it's too hard to do research on a phone, so here we are. Also, we can work together, maybe bounce some ideas off each other."

"Who's this Dan Hansen guy?" said Noah. *Finally, he speaks.*

Jonas began to open his mouth to answer, but I interrupted him before he could let it slip that Dan Hansen was my father. "He's the guy who killed the girl whose photograph was left with Allison." I gulped. "And Rebecca."

"Oh," was all he said as he looked down. Although he looked mournful, he looked more invested than he had before, as if he had a newfound purpose.

I typed furiously, trying to accomplish as much as possible before my mom realized that I had left the house. I typed the username into the search bar and started scrolling. "So what's our goal today?" Jonas questioned.

"I'm going to try to search for blogs and websites that he—"

"Or she. Don't be sexist, Haley," interrupted Jonas.

"Beside the point. I'm trying to look for all the blogs and websites that he, or she," I added for Jonas, "could be on to try to find other accounts. I'm thinking that maybe they'll give us some type of insight into what these people think like. So that we might be able to, you know, have an easier time looking for the killer. Maybe they might even be on one of these blogs."

Jonas and Noah shared a worried glance. Saying it out loud made me realize how far-fetched that sounded. "You know what, never mind, guys. This is stupid," I said. But when I tried to close the laptop, Noah's hand blocked it.

"It's not stupid. Maybe a little out there, but it's the best idea we have. What else are we going to do?"

"He's right," Jonas interjected.

"Okay," I said shyly as I propped the screen back up again. The first thing we looked at was a Tumblr post. But it had a lot of negative feedback, so we decided to look for comments defending Dan Hansen and websites where people supported him.

After about half an hour of digging and a few iced coffees to keep our spot, we finally found something. It was an obscure website where an account was allowed to post a prompt and other accounts could respond in a blog format with text and photos. *Jackpot.*

This post was by someone with a similar username, but we couldn't be sure it was the same person. They'd written: "What are you doing to spread Dan's message and make sure it doesn't die in vain?" The responses were along the lines of "lol" or "is this a joke?" But there were also many that were a little more radical. Someone posted a picture of a GoFundMe they'd set up to free Dan Hansen. *What do those sickos think raising money is going to do? Bring Hannah back and solve world hunger?*

I was scrolling through the posts so fast I almost missed it. Another photograph. A strangled gasp escaped my throat, and Noah and Jonas gave me a weird look as my hands flew to my mouth.

This photo was different. The other ones were screenshots of websites and posters people had made, many of them sick jokes. This one appeared to be a photo of a photo. But what was scary was that it was one I'd seen before—one that was next to me every morning when I woke up, except for the past few days.

The familiar photo glared at me, Hannah's crossed-out eyes burning deep into my soul and mocking me for letting two more girls die.

I clicked on the photo and furiously zoomed in to be sure of what I was seeing. Unfortunately, my eyes were not deceiving me. It was the real thing—the photo that had been stolen and left with Rebecca's body. Perhaps it wasn't her that took it. But maybe she did. Maybe the killer took it after they stabbed her. There were so many *maybes* and *what-ifs* that I felt I could never be sure.

I was speechless for a full minute. I knew I'd have to come clean. "Are you going to tell us what that is?" asked Noah.

"Yeah, one sec," I replied. I had completely forgotten that I was in the photo. *Shoot.* I'd have to tell Noah sooner or later, but I wasn't sure now was the best time. There aren't many things worse than having someone kill your friend and then having your other friend tell you she's been lying to you for months.

I covered my face with my hands and leaned back in the booth. And to everyone's surprise, even mine, I started laughing. Through the cracks between my fingers, I could see the other people in the cafe start to look at us.

Jonas tapped my knee with his. "Haley, shhhh."

I took my hands off my face and looked at the ceiling in an attempt to keep both the laughter and the tears at bay. In the last week, I was sure, I had cried more than most people. I didn't really want to surpass my own record this week. "Sorry," I said. Noah rolled his eyes.

"Explanation, please, Haley," he said.

"Yeah, okay." I was at a loss for words. "That's what was left with Rebecca's body. Whoever posted that is our killer."

Jonas and Noah were speechless too. After a moment of awkward, concerned silence, Noah finally said something. "What's the username?"

I squinted to look at the username. "FlyingMonkeys," I said finally. *Huh.* It was an oddly childish name for a serial killer.

"Hm," was all Noah said. Jonas said nothing.

"Any idea who FlyingMonkeys might be?" I asked them. "You've been here longer than me. Does anyone else use that as their username for anything?"

"Let me check," said Jonas as he took his phone out of his pocket and scrolled through his contacts. "Nope," he confirmed. Without warning, Noah grabbed the laptop. "I gotta go, but before I do, you need to explain something to me, Haley." He looked me dead in the eyes. All traces of the warm, comforting Noah I had known a week ago were completely gone. What was left was a shell of him. Paler, less talkative. Altogether less. "Why were you in the picture?"

"I knew the girl Dan Hansen killed. He's my dad. I'm sorry."

"Better late than never," he said, shocking us both. "I'll call you later. There's just something I need to do." And with that he left, walking off in the opposite direction from his house. I wondered where he was going.

"What was that about?" I asked Jonas. Noah's words haunted me. They were so similar to what Rebecca had said to me before she'd left. What did he need to do, and what did Rebecca have to do? Maybe it was paranoia, but you could never be too cautious. Especially now.

"Beats me," Jonas said. Still, he looked unsettled. I sensed that he knew more than he was letting on. "What now?" he asked nervously.

"I don't know," I answered. "More coffee?" Rebecca and Allison's deaths, and Hannah's, had consumed my every waking moment since what seemed like forever. I needed a break.

Maybe my mom was right: I should just keep my head down and let the detectives take care of the case. But there was still that little nagging voice in the back of my brain that told me not to trust anyone. The police were desperate to find a murderer, but were they desperate to protect me and my mom? It didn't feel like it. It felt more like they were trying to put me in the frame and wrap this up with a neat little bow. A daughter of a murderer moves to town. Murders. Gets arrested for murders.

"I'll take care of it," offered Jonas. "What's your order?"

"Um ..." I trailed off. "Surprise me," I decided as I smiled at him.

"Sure thing." Jonas looked at the chalkboard detailing the different options before getting into line.

It wasn't too long, maybe five people, but it would give me enough time to text Noah without drawing suspicion from Jonas. *What was that about?* I texted him. He was quick to reply. *Call me later* was his response. That didn't help me at all. It was pretty much exactly what he had said before leaving. But after a minute, my phone buzzed in my pocket. *Stay safe*, Noah added. The tiny hairs on my neck stood up with that final message. It was what he had said to me just days after Allison had died.

"Whatcha looking at?" Jonas asked when he came back, with two mugs in hand. He startled me and I jumped, eliciting a chuckle from him. "Don't worry, it's just me. Here's your mystery drink." He handed it to me.

The contents of the white mug were ... mysterious. "Are you sure this is coffee?" I asked half jokingly. The mug was filled with a dark liquid that was covered in weird amber foam. It looked like it was glowing.

"It's their best stuff," replied Jonas. "At least, according to Cool Beans. I've always had my doubts about this place."

It tasted earthy but also like coffee. Unfortunately, not good coffee.

"Mmmm," I mumbled. It had a sour aftertaste, causing me to scrunch my face up. "What is this?"

"Almond bean cream foam," he revealed.

"Bleggh. That explains a lot. I'm like ninety-five percent sure that almonds don't even have beans." I put my mug back down on the tabletop. "So what next?" I asked him. "I've lived here for a few months and this town is painfully small. But I haven't gone anywhere." I paused. "I mean, what do people do for fun around here?"

"I have just the place," Jonas said mischievously as he poured his coffee into a metal water bottle. "Do you want to bring yours too?"

"No, thanks. I'll pay you back," I turned to pull a few dollar bills out of my purse.

"No need," he said. "Consider that wonderful drink my treat." I laughed as he extended his hand to me. "Let's go."

"So where exactly are we going?"

"It's a surprise," he replied playfully.

"It better be more exciting than that coffee."

He guided me out the door and back in the direction of the school. "It's a little ways away, but not too far," he said. "Are you scared of the dark?"

"Depends on where I'm standing," I said as we walked hand in hand towards the woods.

23

We made our way up the stream in the opposite direction from the crime scene, and it turned out to be a decent hike. The trees were a lot thicker by now, creating a beautiful canopy above us. When we were a long way into the foliage, Jonas asked me to close my eyes. The air had grown much cooler.

"Okay, you can open them now," Jonas said, his voice fading.

I removed my hands from my eyes and blinked but saw nothing. I was engulfed in complete darkness and completely alone. "Jonas?" I asked the darkness. My voice echoed back at me.

Where am I?

"Jonas," I yelled.

Suddenly a bright flashing light blinded me and I covered my eyes. A high-pitched wail escaped my throat. I blinked furiously, trying to adjust to the light. When I came to my senses, I was utterly amazed. I was surrounded by thousands of stars. Not real stars, of course, but star lights. They covered the ceiling of wherever we were, making it seem like we were in outer space. I looked around. Jonas was leaning against the lumpy gray wall, a metal box in his hands, probably the light switch. "Where are we?" I asked, twirling around to admire the handiwork.

"You know Vepar tracks?" That I knew. It was the long railroad line that signaled the far northern border of the town. It rolled over the only hills in town, and when the freight trains rumbled across, they made a loud, throbbing vibration like a herd of elephants passing through. "We're under it."

"Under it?"

"Yeah. It turns out there's this little cave-tunnel thing under one of the hills. It's pretty much abandoned, so I did this. This is where I go when I want to be alone."

"Woah," was all I could say. I looked up at the ceiling of the cave. The canopy of lights wasn't the only thing that amazed me. There was a solar system, complete with all the planets. I didn't know what they were made of—papier-mâché, maybe—but they glistened. "I love it. Why did you bring me here? I mean, if this is your special place. It's amazing, really."

"It doesn't feel special if you can't share it with anyone, right?" He smiled. "You're the first one."

I turned around to face Jonas, smiling like an idiot. "Really?" I asked. "Not even Noah?"

"Not even Noah," he confirmed. He took a step forward, and without warning, he leaned in.

I thought he was going in for a hug, so I leaned in too. He must have been going in for a kiss, because his lips connected awkwardly with my neck. I pulled away and took a step back. Jonas jumped back. "Haley, I'm so sorry. I just thought—"

"No, no, no, it's okay, really," I stammered, trying to catch my breath and think on the fly. *Really didn't see this coming.* "I should get home soon. Thanks for everything. K, bye," I told him in a hurried voice.

And with that I did a fast walk out of the cave. And immediately felt guilty and confused and embarrassed. It's not that I didn't like Jonas, because I did. A lot. But it was just too much happening all at once.

Jonas didn't follow me out, which was a relief. I started sprinting but was soon out of breath. I had been away from home for too long. I checked the time on my phone. 2:30 p.m. I cursed under my breath as I walked back home as quickly as possible.

Luckily, I was there before my mother was. She hadn't even texted me about my whereabouts yet. *Thank God.*

I let myself fall on my bed, breathless. Despite all of the coffee, I was exhausted, but I knew I'd never fall asleep with this much on my mind.

I stared at my phone in an attempt to distract myself from the jumble of thoughts bouncing around in my head. I scrolled through my Instagram and Snapchat. I hadn't been on Snapchat for at least a week and Instagram for even longer. By that logic, Instagram would have more to help distract me, so I started there. The only things that flooded my feed were screenshots from the school's website about another memorial for Rebecca.

I sighed and was about to turn off my phone when I remembered that I had to call Noah. I went to his contact, pressed the phone icon, and held it to my ear, waiting for the tone. "Hello?" Noah's voice suddenly answered.

"It's Haley."

"I know that. You're in my contacts." There was an awkward pause for a moment. "Thanks for calling."

"No problem. Why'd you need me to call you, anyway?"

The silence mixed with static as I waited for Noah's reply. "Because I've seen that girl before, in the picture. I just didn't want to say anything in front of Jonas."

"Where do you recognize her from?" I tried to keep my tone calm and low, but even I could hear the panic in my voice. *Has he met Hannah?*

"It's weird, actually. I didn't realize that she was Hannah Schulz when you told us about the first photo a couple of days ago, because, you know, we didn't actually have it. But it was a few weeks ago. I was meeting up with Rebecca at her locker for tutoring. Allison and Sarah were there too. When Rebecca saw me, she walked over, but when she turned her back to them, I was close enough that I saw Allison hand something to Sarah. It was a picture of that Hannah girl."

"What? Why?"

"I'm not sure," Noah said. "But they seemed really secretive about it, like they didn't want Rebecca to see it."

"Why wouldn't they want Rebecca to see? She was their friend too," I asked. But then I remembered that Rebecca had told me that Allison had been distant from her lately.

"I didn't know Allison well, and I don't know Sarah. But maybe Sarah got Allison involved in some kind of online weirdness, and she didn't want Rebecca to know because she would have told them how stupid they were being."

"Okay, thanks for telling me. I'll see you tomorrow at the memorial, right?" He confirmed this and we said our goodbyes, and I hung up. The call might have ended, but my spiraling thoughts had not. My mind was so confused, it was on the brink of surrender. What did Allison and Sarah have to do with Hannah? Why wouldn't they tell Rebecca? And the big, dark, ugly question: how did all this misery find me in Fort Vepar?

I didn't know anything except that the only person with any answers was Sarah.

24

On Sunday, I arrived at Rebecca's memorial early. Two dead girls in a small town in one week. One was cause enough for a big story; two was a recipe for a media frenzy.

I wanted to talk to Sarah before the cameras showed up. Sure enough, she was right outside the school. She was sitting on one of the cement planters leading up to the entrance with a stoic expression on her face.

"Hey," I said as I walked up to her. "You're here early."

"What do you want?" she spat at me. I was taken aback. I had pegged Sarah as kind of rude, but not hostile. Once again, I wondered why everyone seemed to have it in for me and why. But I knew Sarah could start unraveling this mystery for me. She was neck-deep in it.

"Whatever." Two could play at that game. "I need to talk to you."

Sarah sighed. "Fine. The bathroom and locker room are the only things open. Do you mind?" I shook my head. She stood up, dusted her long black coat off with her hands, and turned to walk into the school, not even bothering to acknowledge me. I was annoyed, but I followed her anyway.

My anger was starting to build. Somehow, this girl had got involved in something that centered on my best friend's murder. I had to get focused and get some answers.

We walked to the girl's bathroom and then into the locker room. Sarah slammed the heavy door behind us and we were alone. The tiny hairs on my arms and legs stood up. She turned to me and raised an eyebrow. "So?"

I was suddenly at a loss for words because I didn't know which of the millions of questions to ask her. I decided to go for shock and awe and not waste any more time.

"Why did you have a picture of Hannah Schulz? And what were you hiding from Rebecca?"

"I don't know what you're talking about," Sarah said, but her face betrayed her. She suddenly turned red and her hand flew up nervously to brush her hair back. She knew more than she was letting on.

"Don't play dumb with me. You and Allison, what were you doing with that picture?" I asked her again, trying to keep my voice flat and empty of anger. It wasn't easy. But all I wanted was the truth.

"Who are you, a cop?" Sarah nearly yelled at me. For all her defensiveness, she was rattled. Her glossy black hair was askew and her eyes wild. When she saw that I wasn't letting go, she went on, "It's none of your business. It's between me and Allison."

"In case you haven't remembered, Allison is dead. You owe her and Rebecca this." It sounded harsher than I had meant it to come out.

"Maybe, but I don't owe you anything," she hissed at me. "Besides, why don't you ask your psycho friends?"

Sarah stormed out and slammed the door in my face. I tried to follow her, but my heeled boots slowed me down. By the time I had reached the entrance of the school, she had disappeared into the crowd.

I took a deep breath and tried to calm myself down. I was already attracting too much attention, as I was breathless and sweaty. I tried to disappear into the crowd, pulling out my phone as I walked. *WHERE ARE YOU*, I furiously typed to a group chat with Noah and Jonas.

behind you

I whipped my head around to find Noah laughing at me.

"Not funny," I said as I walked up to them.

"Sorry. You looked like you were on a rampage, so we didn't stop you," said Noah, trying to stifle a laugh. Jonas kicked him in the shin. "Ouch, dude," he muttered under his breath. "Fine, sorry."

"I just talked to Sarah," I whispered to them, but not before looking around to make sure that no one was watching.

"Really?" asked Noah way too loudly. Jonas kicked him in the shin again. "Seriously, dude, stop kicking me," he said. "What did she say?" he whispered much more quietly this time.

Jonas looked confused and a little bit annoyed to be out of the loop. *Is he ... jealous?* "What are you guys talking about?" he asked.

"Can you catch Jonas up?" I asked Noah.

"Fine," he said. "I saw Allison hand Sarah a picture of that dead girl when Rebecca wasn't looking. But, like, a couple weeks ago."

That dead girl. Ouch.

Jonas's face grew beet red. "Why didn't you tell us this, like, a week ago?" He jabbed at Noah as he spoke.

"I didn't know it was her until I saw the picture yesterday. I wanted to be completely sure," Noah shot back.

"Yeah, but it's still weird you didn't mention it. What the hell?"

"Guys," I interrupted. They both turned to me. "Now's not the time."

"But I'm not wrong, right?" Jonas persisted.

Neither Noah nor I responded. It was true, he should have told us earlier, but there were things I should have told them earlier too.

"And keeping me out of the loop, guys? Not cool. I thought you wanted my help, but I guess not."

"We do," I interjected before he could start ranting. "Noah just wanted to be certain. He was really doing *us* a favor."

Jonas's anger seemed to dissipate. "Fine," he grunted.

Right then, Mrs. Donahue opened the outer doors to the gymnasium and started ushering everyone inside. The layout was exactly the same as it had been for Allison, and I had a sudden gut-wrenching feeling of déjà vu.

This time it was Rebecca's portrait on the stage and her weeping family. The rest was a blur, though I do remember Sarah giving what I swear was the same speech that she'd given at Allison's memorial.

I left the building feeling much worse than when I'd entered. There was tension among our group, but for the first time in ages, it wasn't because of me. Noah and Jonas glared at each other as we walked out of the gym. We had decided to go to my house afterward to regroup.

Then it occurred to me, I hadn't told Noah that Jonas had tried to kiss me. In fact, I had been so lost in my own head that I'd almost forgotten it myself. I suddenly felt very awkward being in the room with both of them. It felt dishonest. I was still a little confused about how I felt, but a more immediate concern was how it was going to affect our little gang.

Things could get awkward.

So we went back to my place and sat in my room for a couple of hours, accomplishing nothing. I made up a need to hang out with my mom and told them we could try again tomorrow. Jonas said he had to get home and bolted across the lawn. Noah lingered behind and was just starting to leave when I called him back in. "I need to talk to you," I told him. He looked perplexed.

"Sure. Am I in trouble or something?" You could tell he was trying to make a joke, but he was still anxious.

"Yes," I said, feigning anger. For a second he looked stressed, but seeing me break a smile seemed to make him settle down a bit. "Do you think Jonas's been acting kind of weird lately?" I should probably have said "different" instead of "weird." Was it weird for Jonas to want to kiss me? Not really. I mean, who wouldn't want to kiss me? Hah! But it was all so sudden.

Noah mulled the question over for a moment. "Yeah, but I can't quite put my finger on it."

"Try."

"Okay, well, for one, he's infatuated with you."

That is weird.

"He tried to kiss me yesterday," I blurted out. *Why did I do that?* Partly surprise. I'd truly had no idea Jonas felt like that about me. It came as a shock, but not an unpleasant one. "You really think he's infatuated? With me?"

Noah's face grew intense. "Really? I mean, really he tried to kiss you? And yes, he really does feel that way about you. So what did you do?"

"I swerved," I replied. "I'm fine with it, it was just awkward. Have you noticed anything *else* strange about him lately?"

Noah bit his bottom lip. "He's been a lot more distant than usual, but that's to be expected, with everything that's going on right now. But it's him insisting on hanging out with you all the time that's concerning me. Not that I'm jealous or anything."

Okay. Never thought you were.

"Okay, then why does it concern you?" He wasn't making much sense to me. Didn't he want us to be friends?

"Yeah, but people have told me that Jonas can be, I don't know the right word for it, intense? I totally get it, but people have been spooked by it in the past. I've always just thought that it's because he's super shy and they're surprised when they get to know him. But he's a really great friend."

"Anything else?" I asked. I hated that I had to keep having these conversations and that none of us were being completely honest with each other. For once I just wanted everything out in the open.

"Not really. I guess he's been staying up really late the past couple of weeks. I get odd texts at three in the morning, which isn't like him. But everyone's been off lately."

I nodded. "Okay. Thanks for telling me. See you tomorrow."

"See you tomorrow," he said before walking off into the night.

25

It was the day of Hannah's memorial. I didn't want to go. For the past week, I'd been having constant panic attacks and not even bothering to check my phone. I didn't want to read all the things people were saying about me, and I had a feeling that they wouldn't hesitate to go off on me in person either. I didn't want the memorial to be about me. I wanted it to be about Hannah, as it should have been. But my mom said it was the right thing to do. Even though some part of me knew she was right, it didn't make it any less difficult.

As soon as I walked through the door, I realized that going had been a mistake. People around us were aggressively trying to make eye contact with us like they wanted us to know the full extent of their hatred. They weren't looking at me, they were looking at Dan Hansen's daughter. I kept my eyes down so as not to make contact with them or let them know how much their hatred mattered to me.

A familiar platinum blonde head stood out among the sea of black. Claire. She sauntered over to me. She reminded me of a cat; cool, calculating, and something disturbing in her eyes that I couldn't quite place. Or maybe it was just the eyeliner. Whatever it was, there was something about her that I didn't like.

She walked right up to me and stood just inches from my face. "You shouldn't be here," she hissed. She was so close to me that I could practically taste her.

"And why's that?" I said back at her, fixing my posture so that I looked almost as tall as her. Although I knew that everyone was thinking it, there was no need for her to remind me.

"It's your fault and everyone knows it." She took a step forward, managing to get even closer to me. "Deep down, you know it too. Stop trying to hide it from everyone. Just admit it."

I didn't want to listen to the rest of what she had to say. I grabbed my mother by the sleeve of her coat and dragged her out of the funeral home.

Because this wasn't supposed to be about me. It was always supposed to be about Hannah.

26

November 18, 2019

For some inexplicable reason, the school board expected us to go back to school the next day, safety be darned. Everyone seemed ready to move past Allison and Rebecca's deaths like it was just the latest drama. It made you think about what would happen if you died, which wasn't a particularly pleasant thought.

Sarah, for one, seemed to be doing particularly well considering the circumstances.

She had cast herself as the new Allison and had replaced herself and got a new Rebecca and Sarah too. It was sickening. It made me think that maybe she'd killed Allison to replace her and killed Rebecca when she didn't go along with it.

That seemed too outlandish, so I decided to scrap that theory. But that didn't mean that Sarah didn't do it. Maybe her newfound popularity was just a perk.

Whatever the reason, whether she did it or not, Sarah knew something I didn't. And for some reason, she wouldn't tell me. I needed information, and badly. I had come to a roadblock. At this point, I didn't care how bold I needed to be to get information out of Sarah as long as no one got hurt.

Summoning all the confidence I had left, I walked up to Sarah when I got to school that morning. She was standing around with her new group of wannabes while she looked at her phone, her puppy dogs marveling at her presence, practically jumping up and down to get her attention.

"Hey, Sarah," I said with a smile, as if we were good friends. Her new girls glanced at each other and then gave me a bewildered look like they couldn't believe that I had the audacity to just talk to Sarah without permission.

"What do you want?" asked Sarah in an annoyed tone. She didn't even bother to look up from her phone.

"Not much. I just wanted to see that Hannah Schulz picture real quick." Sarah slung her backpack over her shoulder and reached into her front pocket. At the last moment, her hand froze and then hovered over the zipper. She snapped her head up to me with her mouth almost comically agape.

"I'm just getting a lip gloss," she quipped. *Sure, Sarah, sure.*

"Okay, thanks. That's all I needed to know." I turned my back on them and began to walk away to my locker to meet Jonas and Noah. Out of the corner of my eye, I could see the new girls giving Sarah weird looks.

"Who's Hannah Schulz?" one of them asked.

"Don't worry about it," Sarah told them. She flung the backpack back over her shoulder and started walking furiously in my direction. *Perfect.* She grabbed my arm with one of her bony hands and dragged me to the side of the hallway. "Come with me," she hissed through her teeth. She guided me out the door and along the side of the school with her claws still grasped tightly around my arm.

When we stopped, I decided to take a dig at her. "What do you want, Sarah?" Her face was beet red and furious.

"What do you think you're doing?" she screamed at me silently. "You can't go around saying stuff like that in front of people. It's immature."

"What's immature is that you won't tell me anything. This is so much bigger than you."

"Yeah, it is, Haley. Just because you have past trauma or something, and I'm sorry that Hannah died, but—"

I cut her off. "Wait. How do you know about Hannah?"

"Don't act like you don't know."

"I'm dead serious." I quieted my voice to a hush. "Be quiet. I can't have people go around saying stuff like that. I've tried really hard to make sure no one finds out about that. I'll never be able to go to college or get a job. My mom will have it just as tough, if not tougher. Don't go around talking about things that you don't know."

Sarah's face continued to grow redder. "Well then, maybe you should have thought about that before you sent Allison all of that creepy stuff."

"What are you even talking about? I hardly ever talked to Allison, let alone sending her 'stuff.' That's just weird."

"Wait, so you didn't send her anything?" Sarah's expression went from mad to confused.

"No," I said in a hushed voice. "I don't even know what you're talking about."

"Come with me," Sarah said without hesitation. She began to speed walk off in the opposite direction of the school while looking down at her phone.

"Sarah, wait. What about school?" I asked her. I was walking so fast to try to keep up with her that I was almost out of breath. Yet she didn't make a sound.

"It's fine," she said. "We're grieving." She didn't even bother to look at me while she said this, still typing furiously away on her phone. "Here," she said and handed the phone to me. "I just texted my mom that I'm not ready." I shook my head at her.

"It's good," I told her. "I have my own." I knew I could call my mom and tell her that I wasn't ready. Still, it was a truth that felt like a lie. A pit of dishonesty grew in my stomach. I also couldn't help but silently judge Sarah for weaponizing her friends' deaths like that.

Nevertheless, I whipped my phone out of my pocket. *Bad cramps*, I texted Mom, *had to go home early.* She probably wouldn't see the text until her break. By then it would be too late to do anything about it.

Sarah was a few feet ahead of me by now. I had to sprint just to catch up to her. I had no idea how it was humanly possible for such a tiny person to move so fast. "Where are we going?" I asked her.

Without missing a beat, "The woods," she replied.

I stopped in my tracks, and for the first time, Sarah put a pause on her powerful stride. With a confused look on her face and her head cocked to the side, she asked, "Why not?"

"Because that's where Rebecca was found. I'd rather talk in a public place."

Sarah rolled her eyes. "So now you think I did it?" she said. When I didn't reply, she said, "Fine. Dash's Diner it is, then." She sighed.

She took off with her familiar stride for another block until we reached the greasy spoon. We slid into the booth in the farthest corner and ordered a small fry to avoid getting kicked out.

"So?" I asked her after a few minutes spent watching her bang away on her phone.

She finally put her phone on the table and leaned in, but not before looking around to make sure everyone was out of earshot. "About a month before Allison died, she started getting all of these weird messages."

"Weird? How so?" I asked.

"At first it was just love letters and stuff like that, which wasn't too out of place. It wouldn't be the first time." It made sense; Allison was pretty much universally adored by Fort Vepar High School. "But then ..." Her voice trailed off. "They just got really strange. Threatening."

"You're not making a lot of sense. You have to tell me everything," I whispered.

She looked uneasy. "Fine." She shifted her weight in the booth and looked around a bit more. "The love letters started showing up for a couple of weeks. Someone kept slipping them into her locker. And we were like, 'Okay, whatever.' She was dating Steven and was like, totally in love with him. But I was like, 'Okay, Allison, they're not stopping, we might as well have some fun with it.' Allison didn't really want to do anything about it but just kind of went with it," she said. "We never told Rebecca about the letters, but I think she could tell there was something else going on. Allison didn't want to upset her."

"What do you mean that you guys 'had fun with it'?" I knew she was trying her best, because she was like me; trying to find that perfect balance between revealing not too little and not too much.

"We wrote love letters back and stuck them in the grate on her locker so the person would pick them up. And then she got a burner phone and put the number down for them to text."

I held my mouth agape. That seemed ... cruel? I understood that it was a prank, but knowing myself, I knew that I would never take something that far. It kind of tainted my opinion of Sarah even further.

"So this 'mystery lover' started texting us, so of course we started texting them back just to mess with them. This happened for like a week, but it must have weighed on Allison's conscience, so she eventually confessed." Sarah stared down at the table.

"And that's it?" I asked. That was hardly a reason to murder someone. But then again, there aren't really a lot of good reasons.

"No," she said, then paused. "Then something else happened. He started sending her pictures of that Hannah girl. Saying that Allison was just like her. It was really creepy."

Sarah paused for a second with her eyes closed. She sniffled, but no tears came out. She wiped her nose on her wrist and continued. "The last few days before, Allison just got really distant. She refused to tell me what the person was saying and sending to her. She shut down completely and refused to talk about it."

"Did you keep any of the paper letters?" I asked. It was a decent place to start. Even if I couldn't get the letters that he—or she—had sent back then, I could at least see how bad the love letters were to get a better idea of how angry this person was. It could certainly have given them a motive. Maybe they were even the killer.

Sarah shook her head. "Allison wouldn't let me keep anything." Then she leaned back and stared off into space for a moment. "Actually, I have an idea."

I leaned closer to her, intrigued. "What is it?"

"Allison was a meticulous planner. Not a lot of people know this about her, because she told us not to tell anyone. She kept everything. Scrapbooks, screenshots, you name it. She even had a box under her bed where she kept old letters and stuff like that. She was really sentimental, you know? Like, she never wanted to let go of anything. I have no doubt that she would have kept the letters too."

"Okay, but how are we supposed to get them? Wouldn't the police have already searched her room and taken her phone in to do forensic stuff or whatever?"

Sarah shook her head again. "Allison had a second phone. We made another number, remember? Another thing that people don't know about Allison is that she was a mess. Not as a person, but, like, literally. I'd be surprised if the police found anything with all the junk Allison had in her room. She was a low-key hoarder but an organized one." She let out a dry laugh while reminiscing about her old friend.

"Still, how are we going to get it? We can't just break into Allison's house. And why would the killer go after Rebecca if she didn't know anything?"

"Hold on a sec," Sarah said as she popped a fry into her mouth. She was back on her phone again. "Allison's parents love me. If I literally just call Allison's mom and ask to come over right now, she'll probably let me. I'll just tell her that I want to pick up some stuff to remember her by." Sarah relaxed the phone against her ear after dialing the number.

The phone rang for a few moments before an inaudible voice started talking on the other end. "Hi, Mrs. Vos," Sarah said in a sugary sweet voice that I had never heard before. There was a quick mumble in response. "Just wanted to check in and see how you're holding up. How's Melanie doing?"

Sarah looked down at her other hand and started chipping at her nail. After a minute or so, she spoke again. It was starting to feel awkward, like I had just walked in on her using the restroom. "I'm holding up okay. I just needed to take a day off. Everything's still pretty fresh." There was more mumbling. "Yeah, actually, there is something I wanted to ask you. Would you mind if I came over and picked up some stuff? Just to remember her by?" After a moment she said, "Okay. Thanks, Mrs. Vos. Talk to you soon." Sarah hung up the phone and stood up abruptly. "Let's go," she said.

I stood up too, but I was still confused. It was a lot to take in at once. I was starting to see why so many people actually liked Sarah. She could be pretty charming.

"Where?" I asked.

"No one's home right now. Allison's dad is at work all day, her mom's out having brunch with her sister or something, and Melanie's at school. Mrs. Vos said we could stop by before they got home." She started walking to the door without bothering to throw away our fries. She turned back and stared at me. "Well?" she said. "What are you waiting for?"

27

Allison's house looked like a castle—no exaggeration.

It reminded me of the White House. Even in the richest part of Fort Vepar, the house stood out. Apparently, Allison's dad was some big-time lawyer who spent a lot of time out of town, and when he didn't, he worked long nights. Sarah said that Mrs. Vos spent a lot of time at the country club and hanging out with the other housewives, so Allison and Melanie got a lot of time to themselves.

According to Sarah, Allison and Melanie could sneak out whenever they wanted practically unnoticed. It helped that the Voses didn't have any security cameras, which I found odd for such a big house.

Sarah and I walked up to the huge double door. Sarah bent down and shuffled under the mat for a key. "Not exactly Fort Knox, is it?" she remarked before unlocking it.

The doors opened to an impressive sight—a winding double staircase leading up to the first floor. Sarah looked down at her phone as she nonchalantly walked up. I followed, shaking my head. It was always surprising to me that some people thought living like this was normal, but I guess it must have been all they'd ever known.

Once we were upstairs, Sarah led me down a long hallway. There must have been at least five bedrooms on this floor and God knows how many more on the next floor. The walls of the hallway were like a shrine to Allison. There were photos of her as a baby and a toddler, and pictures of her and Sarah at soccer tournaments. Surprisingly, Sarah made more appearances on the wall than Melanie, their own child. Maybe her photos were on the next floor or perhaps she was just bringing up the rear, so to speak. She certainly didn't seem like the star player in this family.

At the very end of the hall was Allison's room. It had a huge double window on the front of the house, which nearly touched a massive oak tree. "This is it," said Sarah.

Allison's room truly was an awesome mess. Boxes and trinkets and stickers and trophies were everywhere, which at first glance screamed "hoarder." But after standing in the doorway taking it all in, something about the mess seemed in a way to be organized, though I couldn't quite put my finger on it. I don't know what the police did when they went through her things, but I got the sense that they'd taken a look at it and decided they were never going to find any clues there. Or maybe they'd taken everything away and put it back where they found it? I'd have liked to ask Cook and Green, but I didn't plan to.

Sarah walked quickly over to the bed and flung herself under it. I watched with morbid fascination as she rifled about under there and started methodically pulling out brown boxes. After about eight or so, she peeked out. "Ready?" she asked. She pulled herself back out and started looking at the labels on the boxes. "She kept everything. Here." She slid one over to me. "Look in this one." I opened the lid of the box and started shuffling the contents around, looking for the letters.

There was everything in there: ticket stubs, Post-it notes, flashcards. But no letters. "They're not here," I told Sarah.

Her response was to slide three more boxes in my direction. "Check these," she said as she started sifting through the remaining four. After an hour, we hadn't found anything helpful. Sarah exhaled loudly. "This isn't right. I know they're here somewhere."

There was no way we were going to find what we were looking for in this mess. And if Allison didn't want someone to find them, they wouldn't.

Fifteen more minutes and I was starting to get annoyed. My thoughts were interrupted by a loud banging noise. "This is pointless!" Sarah shrieked. Papers and an upturned box lay at her feet. "I feel so stupid. I should have known that we wouldn't find anything."

Being all alone in an empty house with an angry Sarah was starting to make me anxious. I couldn't even be sure that Sarah wasn't the killer. Maybe this was all just an elaborate ruse to get me alone. "Calm down," I told her. You could practically see the irritation boiling under her skin. "Is there any place where Allison hid things?"

"Like what?" But then her face lit up with an idea. "Actually, yeah," she said. "Don't tell the Voses this," she whispered. Even after Allison's death, Sarah still clearly cared about what the Voses thought of her, almost like they were her parents. "Sometimes I'd make Allison sneak out with me. I needed someone to go out with me just in case something happened." She paused and then pointed at the window. "She always went through there. Her parents never even bothered to put any lock on the window because they didn't think Allison was dumb enough to try to get out that way. The tree's pretty unstable, but Allison had a rope. Here," she said and walked over to the window. It took her a mere second to unlatch and open it. She turned around. "Spot me," she said. "I've never done this alone before."

I nodded and Sarah placed her right foot on the windowsill and hoisted herself up and out. She turned herself outward so that I could only see below her knees. For a moment, I feared that she was going to fall and I extended my arms. Then I heard a rustling noise as she emerged back through the window with a rope in her hand. "This is what she used to use to sneak out."

I looked at the rope. Allison was strong, but I doubted that she would have had the upper body strength to pull herself back up after a late night out. "How'd she get back up?" I asked Sarah.

Sarah pointed to the window again. "Look closer," she said. I squinted my eyes and focused. If she hadn't pointed it out, I never would have noticed. There was a platform built into the upper branches of the tree, maybe the remnants of a treehouse. It was more like a moldy square with a couple of nails poking out. Wooden rectangular steps lined the thick trunk, but those looked unsteady too. Never in a million years would I take my chances climbing that route, but I guess Allison had. "She'd climb up there and swing herself a few feet to get back in the window."

"Wait, what does this have to do with the letters?" I asked. Sarah shrugged, fiddling with the rope. She looked almost embarrassed. "I don't know. I thought that maybe she'd hide something there because no one would ever look." She was right; although it was a bit of a long shot, it made some kind of sense.

"Good thinking," I said, trying to butter her up. "Why don't you go look?"

Sarah looked at me like I was crazy. "What? Are you kidding me? Do I look like I have a death wish?" Her mocking expression faltered for a second. "Not literally. You know what I mean." She paused. "This is your mystery. Go solve it."

I sighed. Just when I'd thought we were jelling.

A long creak sang out from the driveway. Sarah and I looked at each other with shocked expressions and bolted to the window. A small black BMW had pulled up to the house. Allison's dad.

"Crap," Sarah hissed. Then she started pushing me towards the window. "Go, go," she urged.

"What?" I hissed back at her.

"Wait until he comes into the house, then go out the window. He can't know you're here." After we heard the front door open, she pushed me back toward the window.

I knew I needed to leave right away. That didn't make the task of getting from the house to the tree any less daunting. Sarah helped hoist me up on the windowsill and I grabbed the rope with shaking hands. It was only a few feet, and Allison had done it hundreds of times. How unsafe could it be? *Right?*

"Cathy?" Mr. Vos's voice boomed from downstairs. "Anyone home?"

"Go," Sarah mouthed at me and then closed the window, leaving me all alone.

"Just me, Mr. Vos," I heard her muffled voice say. Mustering all the courage I had, I grabbed the rope, half closed my eyes, and took my feet off the sill. I swung across to the tree, expecting the rope to snap or one of a thousand other things to go wrong. But suddenly my feet were back on solid ground. The platform wasn't as rickety as it looked from Allison's bedroom, but it was definitely far from stable. And even better news was the small brown box that had clearly come from the same set as the ones under Allison's bed.

I carefully settled down to a sitting position on the platform and lifted the lid off the box. I planned to take a look inside and leave it there, but then it occurred to me that I might as well just take the whole thing; no one would miss it. I pushed the box into my backpack and gingerly made my way down the tree, and I mean gingerly. The wooden blocks nailed to the trunk were really slippery, and every few steps I would slip a little, which made me hug the trunk with everything I had. But eventually, I made it to solid ground. When I was certain no one was watching from the house, I ran down the driveway and then along the sidewalk without looking back.

28

My mom got home from work a few minutes after I ran through the door. *Perfect timing.* She knocked quietly on my door and then slipped in, in her best mom mode ... sympathetic, loving, caring. "Hey, sweetie, I got your text." She walked over to the bed where I was lying and started stroking my hair. "Is everything all right?"

"Yeah," I told her. Before I could say more, she placed her hand on my forehead, checking for a temperature. "I just had really bad cramps and got nauseous and I couldn't pay attention." I clutched my stomach in fake pain.

"You poor thing. I'm going to let you rest. Let me know if you need anything." I nodded weakly with feigned sickness.

The second the door was closed, I grabbed my backpack and flung myself onto the bed. I clawed furiously at the zipper, trying to get it open as quickly as possible. The little brown box was exactly where I'd put it.

The contents weren't like the others in Allison's room. Those papers were all unwrinkled and orderly, while everything in this box was still crumpled and folded. Was Allison mad at them? I unraveled each piece of paper carefully and placed them in a pile next to me. In true Allison fashion, they were ordered by date. There were even printed copies of screenshots. I started at the beginning.

At first, the letters started out almost sweet but creepy.

Dear Allison,
You probably don't know me, but I know you. I've liked
you for a while.

Then they started to lose their sweetness and got creepier
and creepier.

Dear Allison,
I love the way you twist your hair and bite your lip when
you think no one's watching. You're so cute and you
don't even know it. But I do.

Then just full-on creepy.

Dear Allison,
You're not like them. You're different. That's why you're
so special to me. That's why I'm going to watch over you
forever and ever.

That was when Allison or Sarah started writing back. I honestly couldn't see Allison doing it by herself. The letters seemed
like words that Sarah had put into her mouth.

Dear ?
What do you think is so special about me?

Dear Allison,
I've been watching you and your friends for a long time.
Sarah's jealous of you. They all are. Watch her as care-
fully as I watch you. She's trying to be you, but she's not
special. Not like you are. Rebecca's fake. She doesn't even
like Sarah, but she likes you. I can see why. I like you too.

Dear ?
It's a little weird that you watch me, but I'm flattered.
Let's continue this conversation over text.
234-391-2987

Sarah probably got a good laugh out of that. That was when the texts started. Allison only screenshotted a few things, never the full conversations. Just the highlights ... or lowlights.

Allison: You never told me why I was special.

?: do i need too? i think you already know.

Allison: I wouldn't mind you telling me.

That was the first screenshot. There was one more—a paragraph from later in the week, I assumed. Allison never responded to it. After reading it through, she must have blocked the number and ditched the burner phone.

?: Have you ever heard of dan Hansen? He's something of a revolutionary, but no one will tell you that. he believed in all the right things: honesty, transparency, faithfulness, and above all loyalty. He even killed for these ideals. most people think he's crazy. They mock him. But they're wrong. He killed her for his daughter, to protect her. If he hadn't one more person would have fallen prey to a lifetime of wrongdoing and hurt. Not just herself, but more and more people. he didn't take a life, he saved them. I like you because you're what dan wanted, you're his vision for the world. He killed for you, Allison.

A cold breeze seemed to flow through my body. I couldn't imagine what Allison must have felt. It reminded me of the weird website that Jonas, Noah, and I had found at Cool Beans.

Speak of the devil! My phone buzzed in my pocket. Jonas.

Jonas: question idk anymore, why did you leave school early?

Haley: I'll explain over call. Ft?

Jonas: sure.

I tapped the facetime icon and extended my arms so that Jonas could see my face. After a few beeps, his face appeared on the screen, smiling back at me. "Hey, what's up?" I asked him.

"Not much. You? Just checking in to make sure everything was okay. Noah said he saw you and Sarah run off. What happened?"

"It's a long story," I told him.

"I have the time."

"All right. Should we add Noah to the call? He needs to know this stuff too." Jonas looked hurt, but he agreed anyway. The screen split in two and Noah's face joined ours. He looked a little worse for wear, but to his credit, he still showed up.

"Hey, guys," he said.

"I talked to Sarah today," I blurted out. All of a sudden, blood was pounding in my veins. Finally, progress.

"Yeah. Everything all right?" asked Noah.

"Everything's good. I think we've made a break in the case."

"We?" Noah's smile faded.

"Yeah, me and Sarah."

"Oh," Noah murmured.

"What's wrong?" I asked him. I was confused. Rebecca was his friend. This should have made him happy. He should want to know who did this to her. And Allison.

"Nothing. I don't know. I'm just so tired. I want everything to go back to normal already. I ... I just don't really want to be involved anymore. I can't help you with the case. We should just let the detectives take care of it for now."

Jonas and I didn't say anything. Not that Jonas had said anything this entire FaceTime.

"Um ... okay," I said. To be honest, I wasn't sure what to say. I understood where he was coming from, but I was disappointed in him for giving up so easily. I was tired too. We all were. But there were two dead girls, and everything was somehow related to Hannah. I wanted some answers. "All right, then. I guess I'll talk to you later. See you tomorrow."

"See you tomorrow," Noah said before hanging up. That just left me and Jonas.

"Well," I said. "Didn't see that coming."

Jonas stayed silent.

I frowned. "What? What's wrong?"

He pursed his lips. "Maybe Noah's right." I cocked my head to the side. "I mean, the longer we dwell on it, the more it's going to hurt. I just need a break."

"Okay. I'll talk to you tomorrow, then."

"All right. Bye."

With a huff, I tossed my phone onto the pile of clothes in the corner of my room. I sighed again and allowed myself to fall back onto the bed. Then I realized that I had rested too long. No one ever got what they wanted by sitting around and feeling sorry for themselves. *Unfortunately, Noah and Jonas just don't seem to get that,* I thought spitefully.

I pulled the box closer to my chest and started pulling out what was left. I really wished I hadn't. What was left were a bunch of picture printouts.

The first was a picture of my father and me that had been pulled from a newspaper, which had blurred out my face to protect my privacy. But someone had replaced the blur with Allison's face.

It was scary to look at myself and see someone else at the same time. It made me feel like there was nothing different about us, like we were interchangeable. Under the photo, someone had written "This could be us."

It sent shivers up my spine. And so did the next one and the one after that. The second-to-last one was a collage of sorts, multiple screenshots of the Reddit forums Noah, Jonas, and I had found superimposed into one. The caption underneath read "They understand, I thought you would too." But it's the last one that haunts me the most. It was of Hannah, but like the others, this one had been edited. Where Hannah's freckles had once been, in their place was Allison's clear and creamy skin. It was Hannah, but if you looked at it hard enough, two faces started to morph into one until you couldn't tell them apart anymore. I knew the other face was Allison's. The message at the bottom was worst of all: "I was wrong, you're just like her. And you know what happened to her."

I cried myself to sleep.

29

And then it was Tuesday. I got to school late, but just early enough to get to my locker before my first class. When I closed the door, Jonas was leaning against the locker next to mine. I jumped.

"Hey," he said.

"Hey," I replied. "You scared me." I brushed off my leggings and composed myself. "What's up?"

Jonas bit the inside of his lip like he was considering his next words. "I wanted to say I'm sorry." He stood up straight. "I didn't mean what I said yesterday. Well, I did, but just know that I'm here for you. If you need help, I'll help." He paused. "But we can't expect Noah to. He's just done trying to play detective."

I nodded, and my heart fluttered inside my chest. So I hadn't been abandoned. "Is Noah here today?"

"No," he said. "He's taking the day off, apparently. Maybe we should too."

"But we don't have time," I said. "Whoever killed Allison and Rebecca is escalating. I think they'll do it again. I've seen this happen before and have replayed in my mind over and over again. I can't let it happen one more time. And it all has something to do with Hannah, so eventually it's going to be my turn."

Jonas nodded understandingly. "Okay. What can I do?" Gone was the usual sarcasm from his voice. He sounded completely genuine.

"Just help me and try to understand. Meet me after school?"
He nodded, and I walked off to my first class.

Trying to learn anything had been hard after Hannah died,
but it was pretty much impossible now. Everything between now
and then had made me feel like I was the star of a really bad teen
drama. And I thought that by now the audience must be shaking
their heads at me for all the mistakes I'd made. *How could she
be so stupid?*

So the big question I was asking myself all day in the real
world was *What am I missing?*

-

Eventually, I met Jonas at the rickety old picnic table at the side
of the school. Going into the woods or meeting him by the Rock
seemed a bit too dangerous. As I waited for him, Sarah passed by
with her gaggle of copycats. She waved them off and strode over.
"Did you find anything yesterday?" she asked me quietly. My
mind raced as I tried to decide what to tell her. Eventually I came
up with ... nothing.

"Call me later," I told her. She nodded and walked away,
returning to her new friends.

I caught a glimpse out of the corner of my eye of Jonas walking over. "Hey there," I said.

"Hey." He slid into the seat next to me. "Just me punching
in for work."

I chuckled. "Of course. I don't have friends, I have assis-
tants. I need some advice." I unzipped the front pocket of my
backpack so that he could see a bit of the pictures but not all of
them, and no one looking at us would be able to see what he was
looking at. Jonas gulped. "I found these at Allison's house yesterday. Do you think I should turn them in to the cops?"

Jonas scooted closer to me. "I don't think so. They might
think you staged them because of Sarah. You said you found
these at Allison's house?"

"Yeah. It's not like I broke in or anything, though. They were just sitting in this box in her old treehouse. It's not stealing if no one's missing them." I wanted to take those words back as soon as I'd said them. Jonas scooted a little farther away. It was subtle, but I noticed.

"Let's just be safe. It's always better safe than sorry, right?" He gave me a weak smile and I nodded. Still, I thought about taking the photos to Cook and Green. If it could help them find some type of motive and find the killer, then it would all be worth it.

It wasn't that I didn't trust Jonas's opinion—I just trusted mine a little bit better.

"Okay, sure," I told him. "Nothing makes sense to me. It all adds up, but to what? I need to go home and work on the case."

"No," Jonas said almost forcefully. "You need a distraction. And some fun."

I didn't want to, but it was so hard to say no to him. "I'm intrigued. Go on."

"As great as Cool Beans is, you need a real taste of Fort Vepar."

"If you're trying to get me to go to Dash's Diner again, it's not going to work," I said with a smile. Jonas laughed.

"No, I would never," he said. "I'm talking about Reynold's."

"Reynold's?" I had never heard of it before. It wasn't a chain, so perhaps a Fort Vepar original.

"Yeah. The arcade on Reynolds Street. That's not its real name, just what we call it. It sounds a lot cooler than Steve's Castle of Fun."

"You're right about that," I told him.

"It's fun," he said, dragging out the "n." "Noah and I go there all the time. They have laser tag."

My ears perked up. "Laser tag?" How could he have known the only way to my heart? Hannah and I used to save up money from lemonade stands and play laser tag at the end of each month when we were little. It held a special place in my heart.

"Yep, laser tag. I was thinking the two of us together," said Jonas.

"Is this a date," I asked him jokingly, "or am I the new Noah?"

"Maybe a bit of both," he replied. "Shall we?"

"We shall. Wait." I paused in my tracks. "I don't have enough money."

"Oh, that's okay. I can pay for you."

I shook my head furiously. "No. I can't do that to you."

"No, really, Haley, it's okay. I want to."

He did? This was sounding more and more like a date. "Okay. I'll pay you back. Let's do this."

Steve's Castle of Fun looked exactly as I expected. It was in one of the town's many strip malls, and both of the shops next to it were closed. The inside held no surprises either—exactly like a Chuck E. Cheese without the mouse. Or rat. Or whatever it is. No matter what you did, arcades would always look tacky.

Jonas led me to the entrance for the laser tag. It took up the better half of the arcade, and the manager blabbed to me about how he was planning to expand next door. Like that was ever going to happen. Jonas and I drifted into line with our competition, a group of preteens, just in time for the talk before the next round.

The instructor clapped her hands together enthusiastically. "All right, everybody, most of you know the rules, but I'm going to go over them one more time," she said with a smile. Two of the taller kids chatted with each other in the corner. I could tell they were regulars.

At that moment, I made it my personal goal to eliminate them as soon as possible. The most satisfying thing about laser tag for me was taking down opponents who thought they were so much better than me. "We'll be in teams of two. I see we have …" Her voice trailed off as she tried to count the people in the room. "Fourteen people, seven teams. Each pair will take vests with matching colors. The object of the game is to eliminate the other teams. If you hit them in the chest, back, or shoulder, their guns will be disabled for five seconds. If this happens five times, you will be eliminated. The winning team is the last one standing. Okay, got it? Let's go."

Jonas and I put on matching green vests and watched a video about how we were the last of humanity and had to fight each other to the death. Then we were in the arena. It was a large black room with glow-in-the-dark tape covering the walls and the shields, which were just half walls around the room. There were two raised platforms on either side of the room, and altogether it resembled a maze.

It took me back to a time in my life when people weren't being knocked off by a serial killer who was obsessed with my father. The good old days.

After the buzzer sounded, Jonas and I immediately took the high ground. We hid in the corner, whispering to each other and shooting people when they found us. Each time we were discovered, we ran to a different place, giggling.

Five minutes in, and neither of us had been shot. Haley Hansen, back from the brink to win one last game of laser tag. I'd just pointed my gun over my shoulder, aiming at an orange vest, when a familiar *womp-womp* noise started.

The kid in the orange vest looked at me and sped away. I cursed under my breath. I turned around to find my assailant, one of the kids from before in a purple vest, snickering at me.

He fled the scene before Jonas had a chance to get him. "Stay here," Jonas told me. "I'll be back in a sec." I nodded and crouched in the corner, shielding my chest with the laser gun, as Jonas ran away.

A minute passed. And then another. And then another. I had been shot two or three more times, but I didn't bother to move, because I knew that Jonas would be back soon. I was still alive anyway, so it didn't matter. But another minute passed, and I knew that at any moment, the alarm would sound, signaling the end of the game.

Jonas hadn't come back for me. I sighed as the game ended, bummed that we hadn't won. I walked back to the waiting area alone.

I saw the two knuckleheads in purple vests high five, and the corner of my mouth twitched with annoyance. I sat down on the bench, which was disguised as fake rubble, while I waited for Jonas.

I counted the heads in the lobby. Twelve. He wasn't there. Confused, I walked over to the instructor, who was talking away on her phone, waiting for the next match to start.

"Ma'am," I said.

The woman looked up from her phone, looking annoyed, but slipped the small device back into her pocket. "Yes?" she said. "What can I help you with?"

"Did you happen to see a guy walk out of here? Wearing a green vest?"

"Yeah," she replied. "You Haley?" I nodded. "He told me to tell you that something came up and he's sorry."

"Oh, okay," I replied. I stood around for a moment, not sure what to do. When I figured there was no point standing around waiting for him to come back, I walked across the lobby to hang up my vest.

"Ma'am." It was the instructor calling me this time. "You still have two more rounds left if you still want to play. You can take the boy's rounds too if you want. You won't have a partner, though. You sure you want to head out so early?"

"No, I guess not," I told her as I slung the vest back over my shoulders. I didn't need a partner to get things done. Besides, if Jonas was being so kind as to leave me alone in a laser tag place by myself surrounded by twelve-year-olds, I wouldn't feel a twinge of guilt about putting his money to good use. After all, he'd said I needed a distraction.

30

I got my phone out of my pocket and started texting Jonas as soon as I'd finished my rounds. I'd had fun playing, but it wasn't the same when you were by yourself. And I had the feeling that both the kids and the parents alike were judging me; a teenager by herself playing laser tag when she should have been studying. *Where are you? What happened?* I texted him furiously.

The instant disappointment of being left alone was soon replaced by rage. Why would he have left me? I told myself that there was a reasonable explanation, but even I was having a hard time believing that.

Then my phone started ringing. I assumed it would be Jonas, but it wasn't. It was Sarah. I pressed Accept. "What's up?" I asked her, but then I remembered I was supposed to tell her that I had found the photos. "Oh yeah, I wanted to tell you—"

"Stop," she said. Even though she couldn't see me, I physically stopped in my tracks. "Your psychopath friend just tried to attack me."

"What? Which one?" I yelled into the phone. Some of the parents around Reynold's started to give me funny looks, which, surprisingly, didn't bother me. I was so done caring about what people thought of me at this point.

"Noah. I was walking home near the woods when he just pushed me to the ground and pulled a knife on me. Then someone yelled at him and he ran away."

"Wait," I said. "Are you sure it was Noah? Like, one hundred percent sure? He wouldn't do that."

"I didn't see his face because he was wearing a ski mask, but I'm pretty sure. He was wearing that weird hoodie that he always wears." Sarah's voice was rushed and worried but also angry. *At me?* "Haley, did you put him up to this?"

"What? Of course not. I was just about to call you. I found the photos in Allison's treehouse. All of them." I paused. "How can you even be sure it was Noah? You didn't even see his face."

She huffed. "I just know."

"Where are you now?" I asked her. I wanted to be sure that if the killer was about, she was somewhere where he couldn't get her.

"I'm at the police station, filing a report."

I sighed with relief, then caught my breath. "Wait. Don't tell them it was Noah. You can't be sure. Just describe the person who attacked you and let them find out who it was."

"Why should I?" Sarah said angrily.

"Because if you don't, then I won't let you see the photos." *Checkmate.*

Sarah was silent for a moment. "Fine," she said finally. "I'll pick the pictures up after school tomorrow. Just don't try to pull anything."

I sighed. "All right. Bye, then." I hung up.

I spent the rest of the afternoon sitting in the library and wandering around aimlessly—anything to stay out of the house and be alone with my thoughts. I eventually walked in around five that afternoon, just before my mom got home from her shift. We sat around the kitchen counter, making small talk, trying to pretend we weren't in the middle of a hurricane.

My mind was in overdrive, but I couldn't tell her that. The more normal I acted, the better for both of us.

But I was thinking ... why had someone attacked Sarah, and if it was Noah, what did he have to do with it? I had tried texting and calling him, but it was all crickets so far.

I was tempted to throw some theories out to my mom, but I couldn't bring myself to do it. She was on edge, as was every other parent in town, and it was ten times worse for her because all roads apparently led back to us. I had to keep acting like things were getting back to normal, for her sake.

After we had been sitting around for about half an hour, talking about nothing, my phone started to ring. "Mom, can I take this?"

"Sure," she said with a smile. Even she was believing that I might just be a normal teenage girl who called her friends all night and ignored her parents. Deep down, I knew that was what she wanted.

It was Jonas. I stepped into my room and took the call just before it went to voicemail. "What the hell, Jonas? You walk out on me, then wait until now to call me? What's going on?"

Jonas sighed at the other end. "I'm sorry. I had to leave. I can explain."

I grunted as I eased onto my bed. "Enlighten me," I told him with an edge of spite.

"Sarah flipped out and accused Noah of attacking her."

"Which he obviously didn't."

"Right. And so Noah was freaking out and asked me to come over. I'm sorry, but all Noah said was that he needed my help, and I wasn't sure if he wanted me to tell anyone or anything."

"You couldn't have just told me? I had to hear it from her. Fuck you! I'm hanging up." He tried to protest, but I didn't want to hear it. I had better things to do than waste my time listening to another apology.

I was starting to get paranoid about Noah. I needed to be sure that nothing had happened to him. *Hey, how are you? Just wanted to check up on you,* I texted him. I decided to scroll through Instagram while waiting for a response. Not a thing about Allison or Rebecca. *Maybe my dad had a point. People are terrible.* I shuddered at the thought. I wouldn't be like him. I couldn't.

My thoughts were snapped back to normal by the buzzing in my pocket. Noah. Finally. *Yeah, I'm fine, thanks for asking. Just had some beef with Sarah that I need to sort out.*

I furrowed my brow. What did he mean? Could he possibly have been Sarah's attacker? When Sarah had called me, I'd assumed it was someone dressed like Noah who had tried to stab her. I'd assumed it was the person who'd killed Allison and Rebecca. I didn't think it could possibly be Noah, because Sarah was probably paranoid and seeing what she wanted to see. But now?

Meet at the bench in 15, Noah texted again.

My shoulders tensed up. The thought of going anywhere that wasn't a crowded public place freaked me out. Now I was being asked to meet a friend who might have just gone all stabby on Sarah.

Be strong, Haley, I told myself. I glanced at the door. I could hear the low rumble of the TV from the other room. This wouldn't take too long. My mom probably wouldn't even notice I was gone.

I opened the window as quietly as I could and walked off into the night. It was starting to get late. *Bad headache, trying to get some sleep,* I texted my mom to make sure she wouldn't go into my room and find me missing. I knew she would completely freak out if she did. And with good reason too.

The night was moonless and crisp. There was something about it that just didn't feel right. It was *too* quiet. But I guess that's what happens when there's a serial killer on the loose in a small town. No one would be unaccounted for, fearing that they would be accused or they would be next. And I could be either, now that I thought about it. But I had to push on.

I arrived at the bench a few minutes early, but I couldn't relax until Noah arrived. A weird feeling was nagging at the back of my mind, telling me that someone was watching. When Noah showed up a couple of minutes later, seemingly out of nowhere, he scared me half out of my mind. As per usual, he was wearing a dark hoodie and sweatpants, which made him look very suspicious. "You scared the hell out of me," I told him. "For a second, I thought you were the killer."

"So does Sarah," Noah said bitterly.

Suddenly a few things clicked. Allison and Sarah hadn't told Rebecca about the letters because they'd thought Noah was sending them. He was the creepy friend that Sarah was referring to.

"What happened with Sarah?"

"I was walking home after school and she ran up and just lit into me," Noah said. "She was going on about letters I sent to Allison, and that I was a killer, and I was friends with you because I found out you were Dan Hansen's daughter, and it just kept going on and on. Kinda freaked me out. I've been sitting at home all night trying to make sense of it."

"Ouch," I said. A couple of things went through my mind. First, he apparently didn't know someone had tried to gut her with a knife. Second, the day Sarah and I had spent together hadn't changed her opinion of me.

That was okay, because my opinion of her hadn't changed either.

"You know that's not true, right?" Noah added quickly.

"What's not true?"

"That I wanted to be friends with you because of your dad." I nodded reassuringly, but inside my stomach, a pit of doubt started to grow. Sarah had a point.

Noah had loved Rebecca, not Allison. Sure, he'd wanted her to find some better friends, but that was only because he cared for her. And there was no way he would have sent Allison those creepy letters. And why would he have killed Rebecca? It made no sense. It wasn't right. It couldn't have been him. "I didn't even know you were his daughter until this week. I swear," he added.

"Then why did you become friends with me?" I asked, genuinely curious. I had gone out of my way not to attract attention since I'd moved here. I'd tried to stay in the shadows and keep to myself. And yet I had managed to make friends here despite all that.

"Because you're different," he said. "You don't try to impress anyone. You don't do anything for anyone. Not in a bad way. You're just unshakeable. Like you know who you are in the world and no one can tell you otherwise."

"Thanks," I said. "Lately I've had a lot of questions, and it's nice to finally have some answers. I'm sorry I flipped out on you the other day. I shouldn't have. I found those letters that Sarah was talking about and completely freaked. They were just so creepy."

"It's okay," said Noah. "I have a lot of questions too, but sometimes I don't want the answers. That's what I meant when I said you were unshakeable. You don't give up. You're strong, and I'm not. I should have been a better friend to you in the past week. I'm sorry."

"I'm sorry too," I told him. "Can we just agree that we're friends and there's a lot of crazy crap going on but we're not going to let it get to us?"

He laughed. "Agreed. Come here." I scooted close to him, allowing myself to melt into his shoulder. He was my warmth on an otherwise chilly night.

For the first time in forever, I allowed myself to relax. Noah had my back and I had his. For the next few minutes, things seemed like they were back to normal. We talked about dumb stuff that didn't matter. Not once did I leave Noah's arms. Soon, a buzz rippled through his hoodie pocket. "Darn," he said as he pulled out his phone and looked at the screen.

"What?"

"My mom wants me home. She's stressed about me being out after dark, with everything that's been going on."

I nodded. "See you tomorrow?" I asked.

"See you tomorrow," he confirmed.

We shared a final hug and parted ways. As I walked home, the unsettling feeling returned to me again, but I couldn't quite place it. It felt like a hundred pairs of eyes were on me, judging me.

My steps quickened, and I walked faster and faster until I was running. I didn't like to be alone in the dark, where monsters were lurking and anyone could take you and no one could hear your screams. I felt so alone and uncertain with Noah gone.

Then it hit me. I knew why I felt so weird. Because at the back of my mind, I had known all along. I just didn't want to. When I had asked Noah what he saw in me earlier, he'd said I was different. I had heard those words before because that was what was written on the bottom of one of the photographs. The killer thought Allison was different. Said she was special.

And so was I.

31

The next day at school, I dealt with conflicted emotions. On one hand, I wanted to be able to be friends with Noah, and on the other, I just couldn't shake his comment from yesterday.

I was special. His words and the killer's, verbatim. That couldn't be a coincidence.

I was also still pissed off at Jonas for leaving me at Reynold's. I got to school just before the ring of the bell to avoid everyone. It had been so long since I'd had a normal problem that I had forgotten how hard they were.

Another normal problem awaited me when I got to trig first period. My teacher, Mrs. Mashal, stood in front of the class with a mischievous look on her face. We all knew what that meant. "As you know," she started, "it's been a month since we last changed seats." The class groaned in unison. "All right, pay attention. When I call your name and your partner's, move to a new table. Steven Liu and Alexandria List at table one. Mark Simmons and Stephanie Wang at table two. Haley Hansen and Sarah Rhodes at table three." I sighed, blocked out the rest of what Mrs. Mashal was saying, and walked over to my new table, feeling resigned.

"Howdy, partner," I said to Sarah as we sat down in our newly assigned seats. She groaned and rolled her eyes at me, making not even the slightest attempt to hide her disgust.

Sarah buried her hands in her eye sockets. "I can't believe I have to sit with you," she thought out loud. It was a large class, and Mrs. Mashal was still reading names off the list and would be for a while. Just long enough for a quick conversation.

"And why's that?" I retorted.

"Don't take it personally."

I laughed. "How could I not?"

"You're fine. If anything, a little dull. But your friends are the ones I have a problem with. You are aware that Noah killed them, right? God, you probably even helped. And for one second I trusted you to be careful with the letters, but all along you just wanted them to get all the evidence off your creepy boyfriend Noah."

Was that really what she thought I was doing? I couldn't argue with her when I wasn't sure myself if Noah had killed them. Deep down, I knew he wasn't capable of that. But that was what everyone said about killers. They never saw it coming. I certainly didn't. "He's not my boyfriend," was all I could think of to say.

Sarah let out a dry laugh without even looking at me. "Sure he's not," she said.

For the rest of the day, I just went through the motions. After school, I waited on the bench to see if either Noah or Jonas wanted to make plans. But to my surprise, it was neither of them that showed up at the end of the day, but Sarah. "Did you miss me too much?" I asked sarcastically. Seeing her was the last thing I needed right now.

She glared at me viciously and walked up to my table with fast, angry strides. "No. Tell me what the hell is going on," she spat at me.

I stood up, afraid that if I was sitting, I'd be too vulnerable. I didn't like looking weak, even if I was. "I don't know what you're talking about." I tried to keep my voice steady and confident, but I had to admit that I was nervous. I had never seen Sarah so enraged before.

"You're just like your dad." I wasn't sure where Sarah was going with this or why, but I figured that I'd better keep my mouth shut. "Everyone's wrong about you. They think that you're this innocent, shy little girl because they don't know what you are." In the distance, I could see Noah and Jonas at the front of the school, watching us. But they didn't come any closer. "That's what the cops think too. 'Little Haley wouldn't lay a finger on anyone because of her oh-so-rough life.'" She was becoming hysterical. "You know, at first I thought that Noah killed them, but I was wrong. It was you. How could I not see that? I fell for your act too, Haley, just like everyone. But I won't anymore."

People around us were starting to whisper now. I could feel beads of sweat pooling on the back of my neck. I wasn't good with confrontation.

"Because you're just like him. And that's why you sent Allison the letters. Because you were testing her. You were looking for a replacement for that girl. A good one this time. One that your father would approve of. But when Allison disappointed you, you killed her. And then when Rebecca didn't suit your needs, you killed her too. And then ..." Sarah stopped to take another breath. "You wanted me, but here's the thing about me, Haley. I'm smart, and I saw through all of your holier-than-thou crap. But here's that thing that you're good at: most people aren't like me, and you tricked them. Because you think you're so much smarter than them. But I think that I should help them out, level the playing field, because I'm a good person, unlike you."

I stepped back. Sarah was so livid that I was afraid that if I was too close to her, she would hit me. But she wasn't quite done yet. "I think we should tell everyone, right, Haley? Your little secret. It's the least you could do for us, since you already killed two of us." My head began to pound.

And that was when I snapped. The anger that was boiling in my stomach shot all the way to my fist, which, to my surprise, made contact with Sarah's jaw. The crowd gasped.

Sarah stumbled backward, cupping her jaw in her hands. I was sure that she was faking it just to show everyone what a monster I was. Let's not kid anyone, I have skinny little arms and couldn't have hurt her if I'd tried.

I locked eyes with her. Then Sarah's new replacements walked over to her, making sure she was okay and making a big display of showing everyone what great friends they were.

I walked away quickly so fast I almost started running.

"Haley! Haley!" shouted a voice behind me. Jonas. I didn't slow down to talk to him; I just kept going faster and faster. "Hold up! Wait!" Suddenly I felt his grip on my arm. I turned around.

"What do you want?" I almost yelled at him. I wasn't in the mood for talking. Just yelling.

"She's wrong."

I laughed maniacally. Of course she was; he didn't need to tell me. "I know."

Jonas looked upset. I hoped I hadn't hurt his feelings. "Then don't let it get to you, Haley. You're one of the good ones." With a sad expression on his face, he turned around and started jogging back towards the school. I, on the other hand, went straight home. I needed some time alone to help clear my head. How many times had I thought that recently?

Unfortunately, there is no rest for the wicked. My mom was already on the porch, waiting for me. "Get inside, young lady," she said. Her eyes were nearly popping out of her skull and the rest of her face was furious. "What were you thinking, hitting another kid at school?" I rolled my eyes and walked right past her. But Cook and Green were waiting for me in the kitchen.

I let out a loud sigh. "You too?"

"Sit down," Green said in a surprisingly stern voice. I had never heard him sound like that before. It was the kind of tone that said "You don't want to mess with me." So I didn't. Obligingly, I pulled up a stool and sat down.

Cook's face was equally stern, but that wasn't nearly as surprising. "Haley, it is our understanding that you assaulted Sarah Rhodes today after school."

Assaulted? Couldn't they have just said "slapped"? Or "tapped"? So officious.

"Yes," I told the pair. There was no point lying to them. There would be witnesses lined up around the block to corroborate Sarah's story.

"And why was that?" inquired Cook.

"Well ..." I began. "To be fair, I was provoked. We were in a crowd of people outside school, and she was saying all this stuff about me."

"What kind of stuff?" asked Green.

"Saying that I killed Allison and Rebecca. And that I was just like my father and I wanted to kill her too. But she was too smart to fall for my tricks." I stared straight ahead, not bothering to make eye contact with either of them. I was scared that they would look disappointed. Especially Green. I felt like he had been rooting for me, but I had let him down.

"And was she right?" asked Cook.

"What?" I wasn't sure if I had heard her correctly.

"I said, was she right? Did you kill Allison and Rebecca?"

So I had heard her correctly.

"No," I told them, trying to keep my voice steady to make myself more convincing. It was a funny thing, how you purposely had to act like you were telling the truth when you were, just to convince people that you weren't lying to them. Or were we just trying to convince ourselves? I didn't want to think about it too much. "I slapped a girl. This has nothing to do with Allison and Rebecca. You've already asked me these questions."

"And we have to ask them again, Haley."

"Why? I don't understand." I saw my mother's haunting figure leaning against the doorframe. She looked like a ghost. Looking at her eyes, I could tell she was gone. "What's going on?"

"Haley, before we proceed again, would you like a lawyer? If you are unable to afford one, one will be provided for you." I looked at my mom with my mouth agape, but she returned my shock with a blank expression. *She thinks I did it. She thinks her daughter is a murderer.*

"I have nothing to hide. I don't need a lawyer."

Cook tapped her pencil against the kitchen table. "All right, then. If you wouldn't mind taking a ride with us to the station, we'd like you to stay the night."

32

June 2019

After my mom and I came back from Hannah's funeral—before it had even started—I wasn't quite sure what to do with myself. It had only been a few days since Hannah's death, but rumors had spread like wildfire in Wilake. Rumor had it, I had told my dad to kill Hannah. That I was a psychopath. Some were even saying that my dad had asked me to pick out a girl for him to kill and that I chose Hannah. None of that was true, of course, but that didn't matter.

And worst of all, it wasn't even about Hannah to them. It was about my dad. Those people had grown up with him and, just as I had been, were shocked that he could have done something so terrible.

As much as they hated to admit it, they'd liked him and shaped the person he'd turned out to be. Even though no one was to blame for Hannah's death but my father, it was only human to feel partly responsible; to wonder if there was anything you could have done to stop him. I knew because I had asked myself that question several times a day since her death. By disassociating themselves from the story, they had found it easier to deal with their guilt. Unfortunately, that guilt would become mine.

I was lying on my bed thinking of where everything had gone wrong, when I heard a knock on the door. Hesitantly, I rose from the bed and peeped through the curtain covering the door.

To my surprise, it was Claire. No doubt here to shame me once again. I tried to pretend that I hadn't heard her knock and walked away from the door. "Haley! I can see you," shouted Claire from outside the house. *Crap. She saw me.* I sighed and opened the front door reluctantly.

"Hi, Claire," I said in a resigned voice. She gave me a weird smile that was a combination of condescension and annoyance. I tried to close the door on her, but her bony hand blocked my way. I opened the door again. "What do you want?" I snapped at her.

She raised her eyebrows in fake shock. "Wow, Haley, I didn't mean to upset you. We all know what happens when Hansens get upset." If it wouldn't have proved her point, I would have slammed the door on her. She saw me as an extension of my father, whom she, like me, understandably hated. "I'm just going to say what we're all thinking."

"Go ahead." I knew what she was about to say before the words even left her mouth.

"We don't want you here."

"I know," I told her. I closed the door and locked it. There was no point continuing the conversation. What else was there to be said? I wasn't even mad, just tired, because I knew that as long as we lived in Wilake, that was what everyone would be thinking, even if they didn't say it out loud. That was the night we decided to move. Because that was when I knew that as long as we were in Wilake, it would never stop.

It's funny how you spend so much time trying to please people so that they think highly of you, but in one second, that can all be taken away. It doesn't even matter if you did anything at all, just what people think you did. Thinking about stuff like that used to make me feel powerless, but that was because I gave it power.

That was why I couldn't just stop trying to find Allison and Rebecca's killer, even if Cook and Green and everyone else thought I'd killed them. I had let people make up their minds about me too many times before, and I was done with that. If I just backed down and quit, who would stop it from happening again and again and again? That was behind me. I wouldn't give them that satisfaction anymore.

33

Fort Vepar's police station was even more depressing than I remembered. Its demeanor completely changed when people were convinced you were guilty. The walls were duller, and every interaction seemed hostile.

I waited in the gray-walled interview room. After a while, my emotions turned to a state which I can neither describe as happy nor sad, nor even angry. I just was.

I don't know how long I sat there in a sort of trance, but when I looked up, Cook and Green had materialized in the chairs opposite me. Green placed the metal tape recorder in the center of the table and pressed Record. After he'd identified everyone in the room, he got down to business.

"Haley, where were you the night that Allison was killed?" Cook had her notepad and pen, looking like she was ready to pounce.

"As I told you before, I was asleep."

Cook scribbled down some notes. How much could she get from such a short sentence?

"And can anyone vouch for that?" she asked.

"As I told you before, no. But I did have the tracker on my phone, which you decided to ignore, you know, as I told you before."

Cook let out a tired and slightly exasperated sigh and put her pen and notepad down. She interlocked her fingers and stared at me. "Haley, do you understand that we want this

175

interview to go as smoothly as possible? It would be very much appreciated if you cooperated fully." She said all of this while showing me her forever-condescending smile.

"I am cooperating fully. I'm here, aren't I?" I paused. "Are you even looking into anyone else?"

Cook's smile widened. "Excuse me?"

"Are you looking into anyone else? You know, besides me." I smiled at Cook. Her smile said *It's nice of you to be here*, but her eyes said *I hate you*. "I understand that it's been a week and a half. And I'm the easy arrest. I imagine that your jobs must be on the line right now."

That seemed to make them think. Finally, Green spoke. "What are you getting at here, Miss Hansen?"

"I'm saying that if you arrested me now, it wouldn't cause any waves. I'm a minor, so my name wouldn't be leaked, and even if it was, considering my father, it would be very believable. Someone goes to jail, and you look like the hero. Case closed." I said this as politely as I could and tried my best to keep a cheery face. "Except you wouldn't be, right? You both know I'm innocent. You have no real evidence against me. So you'd be putting an innocent person in jail and the real killer would still be out there, living free. So everyone wins—except for me and the people you know he or she is going to kill in the future."

Green shifted in his seat. Cook, on the other hand, looked perfectly calm. Then there was a hum from Green's bag, drawing all of our attention. He reached down and pulled out a phone. "I have to take this," he said to Cook and walked out of the room.

"It's just you and me now," I told her.

"What a treat," she replied sarcastically.

"For me too," I said. "You know, I could help you. I know things that you don't, but maybe you would if you were a little bit better at your job."

"And what do you know, Miss Hansen?"

"Facts. A decent amount of them too. Maybe enough to help you get somewhere in the case."

"Any chance you could share this valuable information?" she asked.

"Maybe, out of the kindness in my heart. If it'll help me clear my name. Does that sound possible?"

"We'll have to see what that evidence is first."

"We'll have to find out what you know first." Wow, was it possible she was listening to me now? "I have some stuff in my backpack, and there are some things I could tell you," I said.

She brushed her straight dark hair behind her ear and then got up and walked to the door. "Can we get Haley Hansen's backpack in Interview Room 1?" she called down the hallway. I heard the murmur of a reply, and then she came back in and sat down, picking up her pen and notebook. "So how about the stuff that you can tell me?"

"There's this website," I blurted out. "Well, Reddit. It's sort of like a Dan Hansen fan page."

Cook continued scribbling on her notepad. "And how does this help us? There are creeps everywhere, Haley."

"I'm aware. But there's this one user, I forget his username, and he posted this picture. A photo of the picture you found with Rebecca. The one that someone took from my phone." Cook's eyebrows went up. "And then he wrote this whole spiel about how he was doing what Dan Hansen wanted and how we're all cowards and stuff. I'm pretty sure most people thought it was a joke."

The metal door opened slowly and a stout sheriff handed Cook my bag. She slid it across the table. "And the evidence in your backpack?" I unzipped the front pocket and rifled around. I put the photos I'd found in Allison's treehouse into a pile and the friendship bracelet next to it.

I decided to start with the bracelet, thinking it would be easier to explain. "The day she died, Rebecca and I threw stuff in the river. It must have floated downstream, because I found it caught in the sewage drain a few days later. I threw in one of my dad's diaries, but I didn't find that there. It was too big to fit through the drain, so it would have been stuck like the bracelet. So someone must have taken it—probably the person Rebecca said she was meeting, the person who killed her. So the killer will have the journal."

"Okay," said Cook. "And those?" She tilted her head, pointing to the letters and photographs.

"Sarah told me that Allison had a kind of stalker at school that they didn't tell Rebecca about because they thought it was one of our friends. Sarah said that Allison kept everything, so we went to her house, with permission, and I found these on the tree platform outside her house. I didn't tell Sarah that I found them. Allison must have not wanted anyone to see them. This guy started sending her love letters, and then Allison and Sarah gave him a number that he could text as a joke." I handed the papers over to Cook. She flipped through them as I spoke. "Then he started talking about my dad, and Allison blocked him. It must have made him really angry, because then he sent her those in her locker. I think it's the same person who posted the picture on the website."

"This is interesting ..." said Cook, taking notes in her pad. "Well, thanks for bringing this in. I'll talk to my superiors about letting you go tonight." There was a knock on the door, and Green poked his head in.

"We need to talk." Green looked off, like he had just been told that his cat had died.

"Okay. Stay here, Haley. I'll be right back." She pressed Pause on the tape recorder. Green walked over to her and whispered in her ear. They were a couple feet away, so I could hear their conversation if I focused really hard. So I did. And I wished I hadn't. Because I wasn't ready for something like this.

"Sarah Rhodes has been found dead," he told her.

"What?" I burst out, although I hadn't meant to. Cook and Green looked at each other warily and then turned to me. Green made his way back to his chair and sat down slowly. He switched the tape recorder back on.

"Haley, we have just found Sarah Rhodes's body along the river, in close proximity to where we found Rebecca's. We're currently investigating her death as a homicide."

"Oh God," I said as I put my hands over my eyes. I couldn't believe it. I had just punched the poor girl a few hours ago.

"You know this means we're going to have to ask you more questions, right?" Green said. I nodded. Cook, for her part, leaned against the wall with her arms crossed, silent for now. Green pulled his phone out of his pocket and laid it in the middle of the table. He swiped through his pictures until he found what he was looking for. "This was found at the crime scene."

I felt hot bile move up into my throat. "Oh," was all I said. It was similar to the photographs I had found at Allison's house, covered in the same smooth coating. It reminded me of the final photo that the killer had given her, but this one wasn't in the box.

It was Hannah's face overlapped with Allison's, but that wasn't all. Rebecca and Sarah were there too. Underneath the photo, "ALL OF YOU" was written in red permanent marker. "Can you tell us about it?" Green asked.

Cook stepped forward from her corner. "She can. She showed me these earlier." Cook tapped her finger on the photos from Allison's house. "She claims she found them hidden at the Vos residence."

"They're not mine," I told them. Cook took her seat next to Green.

"Well, whose are they if they're not yours?" she asked.

"The stalker I told you about. It has to be him. Or her?" Green gave Cook and me a confused look. Even I could hear the sweaty desperation creeping into my voice. I wanted them to believe me so badly that it sounded like I was lying.

"Okay," she said. She pounded her hands lightly on the table and stood up again. Her anxiety and anger had manifested itself in some type of physical tic.

"Okay?" I repeated. I wasn't sure what she meant.

"One last question." She placed her hands back on the table and stared me straight in the eye, her feet pushing against the smooth concrete like she was ready to spring out of her chair. "Who did Sarah think was sending Allison the letters?"

Now I really began to sweat, not wanting to throw anyone under the bus. "Well, me. That's what she told everyone."

"No, before that. You mentioned that Sarah and Allison never told Rebecca about the letters because they thought a mutual friend was sending them. As you explained, you didn't know either girl very well, so it couldn't have been you. Who was that friend, Haley? Who did they think was stalking Allison?"

I didn't reply. I didn't know if I was physically capable of it.

"Haley, you don't have to protect anyone," Green said softly.

"Okay," I said quietly. "Sarah and Allison thought it was Noah. Noah Johnson."

"Thank you for your cooperation, Haley," was all Cook said before she ran out the door.

Green watched her go and turned to me, shaking his head. "We're done here, okay? I can walk you out."

I nodded and grabbed my backpack off the floor. I left the photos and the bracelet on the table. I was sure they wanted them, and I wouldn't be needing them now.

I started walking toward the door, then stopped. "Wait," I said. "What's going to happen to Noah? He's my best friend. I know he wouldn't do anything like this."

Green rested his hand on my shoulder. "Nothing. We have no physical evidence, so at this point you're just assisting us with the investigation."

But he didn't look too sure about that. Nevertheless, it calmed my nerves a bit, though I was starting to feel in my gut that I had just betrayed Noah.

My mom was standing in the lobby waiting for me. She rushed me to the car without a word and drove fast, which was unusual because she typically drove as slowly as a grandmother. Her eyes were tear-stained and her hair was sticking up at all angles. She was taking on that frazzled look that had dominated the calendar for the past six months.

"Mom?" I said. She didn't take her eyes off the road. "Mom?" I repeated. Still no response. Might as well try again. "Mom!" I screamed. Instead of slamming on the brakes, which would have been a normal reaction, she actually speeded up. Now there was only one way I knew to get her attention. I unbuckled my seatbelt, which is every parent's worst nightmare.

When the alert started pinging, my mom slowed down and pulled onto the side of the road. "Hell, Haley! What are you doing?" Her knuckles were white from gripping the steering wheel.

"What are you doing? Talk to me."

She sighed loudly. "We can't stay here. You were right, we should have left the second that first girl turned up dead. I can't let these police screw you up."

That first girl. Allison. It had begun to happen. The victims no longer had names or stories. They were forever tied to the man who had killed them.

"Okay," I whispered. I felt exhausted, and suddenly the idea of running away from this life was really appealing. "Where are we going? And when?"

"Aunt Linda's in Michigan. She says that we can stay in one of her old rentals because she's not getting much use out of it anyways." My aunt rented out cheap vacation homes, but I didn't know she and my mom were still on speaking terms.

"I thought you hadn't talked to Aunt Linda in months?"

She sighed again. "Family is family, Haley. Nothing can change that. You can't stay mad at each other forever." I nodded, though I was mentally poking holes in that logic. My dad was family and I had no problem not talking to him. And I was planning to stay mad at him forever.

"We leave tomorrow afternoon. Let's go home and pack up, baby, okay?" She pulled the car back onto the road and started to drive home. Home. A sad little house full of big bad memories.

34

Packing would be pretty easy, seeing as I hadn't even bothered to unpack in the first place. All I needed to do was move the boxes from my closet to the car and throw everything else into my duffle bag.

Our moving day took about thirty minutes. But I still had over a day left in Fort Vepar with nothing to do. School was obviously off the table for tomorrow. How was I going to spend my last day in this suddenly wicked little town?

I walked back into my empty bedroom and sat down on the mattress. I lay on my side and turned on my phone. Over fifty messages, which was unusual, but not too much. I assumed they were from angry people blaming me for Sarah. And the rest. It had happened before and would happen again. But to my surprise, they were all from one person: Jonas. I scrolled through them.

Haley?
HALEY
we need to talk
it's about Noah
call me asap

The rest of the messages followed the same sort of pattern. Taking Jonas's advice, I called him in a millisecond. What could have happened to Noah? My heart started racing. Jonas picked up in less than one ring. "Jonas," I said in a rushed voice, "what's going on? Talk to me. What happened to Noah?"

Jonas started talking, sounding like he was in a hurry. "I was walking with Noah down the street just talking and stuff we wanted to come check up on you and then ..." His breathing got even more labored.

"Jonas, slow down."

"Okay, okay, sorry. And then this police car drove by and some cops just jumped out and put him in handcuffs and drove him away. They wouldn't even tell us why. They just took him, Haley. I ..." His voice cracked.

Then I remembered how as soon as I'd mentioned Noah's name, Cook had bolted out of the interview room. "Jonas, stay calm. When was this?"

"A few minutes ago."

It was an hour since I'd left the station. Did they have something on him and didn't waste any time? Or was it something I'd said to Cook and Green? I wasn't sure if I had given them the first piece of a puzzle or the last. I could feel sweat forming in beads on my forehead. "And what did the police officers look like?"

"The one that grabbed him was a woman. Tall, kind of pale. Straight, dark hair in a ponytail. She looked angry. Everything was a bit of a blur." *Cook.* "Haley, I don't know what to do. I'm coming over."

"Okay," I told him. "You need to tell me everything. The front door's unlocked."

"Okay. See you in ten." He hung up.

I put my back against the bedroom wall and slowly slid down, putting my head between my knees as I tried to think this through. There was no way Noah could be the killer. Could he?

Jonas rang the doorbell. I peeked through the slot in the door to double-check it was him and then opened it for him.

"Who's that?" screamed my mom.

"A friend. Be back in a while," I yelled back. I heard her say something back in a louder voice, but I was already closing the door behind us as I pushed Jonas down the porch. He looked confused. "Let's go somewhere else. My mom's in a mood," I said.

"Sure," he said. "The cave?"

I nodded, though a thought in the back of my mind was telling me to be cautious. On one hand, I didn't want to go somewhere secluded; on the other, I didn't want to see anyone else in this town before my mom and I left it forever. Caution was lost. "Okay, tell me everything that happened and I'll tell you my side of the story."

"Your side of the story?"

I cringed with guilt. "Yeah. I'll get to that later."

He looked perplexed but continued talking anyway. "So we were just walking over to check up on you when that police lady arrested Noah and drove away."

"And they didn't tell you why?"

We walked in silence for a while, both thinking that we wanted to save the conversation until we were alone. Eventually, we made it to the cave, ducking as we walked in.

"So what's your side of the story, Haley? You said something about that earlier."

"Yeah, you might want to sit down for this." Jonas leaned against the wall and slumped down into a sitting position. I followed suit. "I think the police think that Noah did it. They think he killed them all."

Jonas twitched. "What? I don't understand. Noah didn't do anything."

"I know," I said. I could feel tears starting to glaze over my eyes and sting. The guilt was overwhelming. "They took me in for questioning this afternoon." I started to choke up. "And I told them everything."

Jonas still looked confused. I hated that I was doing this to him. Wherever I went and whatever I did, the people around me always suffered. And it was all my fault. "What do you mean by *everything?*" Neither of us said anything. "Haley, what did you do?" He looked scared now, not confused.

"They thought I did it, and I didn't know what to say. Jonas, you need to understand." I was crying now. "I told them about the Reddit account and the photos I found and the bracelet. And everything else. All of it. And then Sarah was killed when I was still in custody, and they just let me go." I sniffled and wiped my eyes. "Then the lady who arrested Noah asked me who Sarah thought sent Allison the photos, and I told her the truth—that Sarah thought it was Noah. And then she just bolted out of the room."

"Oh," was all Jonas said. We were silent for a moment. I figured I needed to come clean and tell Jonas everything.

"But here's the thing," I went on. "They must have something on him. The other detective told me that they couldn't arrest or hold him without some type of evidence." My phone vibrated in my pocket, but I ignored it.

Jonas looked up from the cave floor. "Are you implying that Noah might have actually done something?" His eyebrows were knitted in anger. I hadn't meant to imply that I thought Noah had done something, because I knew in my heart that it wasn't true.

"No, of course not. I'm just saying that they have something that makes it *seem* like Noah did something." My phone buzzed again, but I knew it wasn't as important as this conversation right now.

"Haley, he's our friend. Don't you believe in him?" He was practically shouting now.

"I don't know what to believe anymore," I screamed back. It came out louder than I thought it would. I wasn't even mad at him, just upset that he thought I would be so quick to discard my friends. I'd thought he would be more understanding. He knew who my father was; he knew I had trust issues.

"Wow," was all he said. My phone buzzed again. I was starting to get sick of it. Jonas turned his back to me and held his head in his hands.

During the lull, I glanced down at my phone. It was Noah. He must have been out of custody.

Call me.

Where are you?

Haley, I'm serious where are you.

We need to talk.

Haley, I need to know where you are now.

Cave, I texted back.

I looked up and focused my attention on Jonas, who had stood up and started pacing around. He suddenly stopped.

My phone buzzed again. I started to tell him that Noah was texting, but he suddenly let out a dry laugh and looked down at me. "I thought you were better than this, Haley."

I winced. "What do you mean? By the way, Noah's out."

The news seemed to make him even more agitated. "What, so now you believe him? Do you need proof to know your friends? Do you even know what friendship is?" Okay, he wasn't even close to making any sense now. And he was starting to make me nervous.

Jonas suddenly turned his back on me, muttering something to himself, so I took a quick peek at my phone as it buzzed again. *Are you alone?* Noah had texted.

Now I was creeped out. I had told Noah where I was. Was he worried about me, or was he mad that I had mentioned him to the cops and now he was coming to hunt me down?

Why? I texted back.

I was jarred from my thoughts by Jonas, who had spun around while I was texting and stood in front of me, yelling. "I thought you were different, Haley! I thought you were different from them!" His dark eyes, once so attractive to me, were suddenly filled with hate. He started to walk towards me slowly.

"What? Different from who?" I stood up with my phone in hand and started backing away from his anger. I wasn't concerned or confused anymore—just scared.

My phone buzzed again, and I glanced down at it.

Are you with Jonas? Noah texted.

A chill slid down my spine.

If you are, run

Suddenly Jonas was right in front of me, our foreheads almost touching. "You don't need to look at your phone anymore," he said softly.

I began to cry. "Oh God, Jonas, what did you do?"

Then my phone started ringing. My hands were shaking too much to actually press the screen, but I could see it was from Noah.

"Put it down!" Jonas shouted.

My phone dropped from my hand. All my strength was suddenly gone as I tried to process what was happening. Jonas. It was always Jonas.

"Why?" I asked as tears rolled down my cheeks. Why was I crying? For me? For the girls he'd killed? Fear?

"Why not?" he said and laughed menacingly. "I thought you'd understand. You're his daughter, after all."

Suddenly, I stopped crying. His daughter? He thought I would understand? The fear disappeared, replaced by a weird calmness mixed with anger. I wasn't going down without a fight. I was going to fight. For the girls he'd killed. For Hannah. Armed with that resolve, the best thing I could do now was to keep Jonas talking. Noah knew something was up. He would come for me. He had to come for me. He just had to.

If he didn't, I was as good as dead.

"What would I understand?" I asked Jonas.

"He was right, you know. We don't need everyone, Haley. Deep down, I know you know that's true."

But I didn't. I knew that wasn't true. No matter how much someone hurts you, they don't deserve to die. "But why did you kill Rebecca? She was your friend. And Sarah. And Allison. Why them?"

Jonas gave me an incredulous look. "You don't know? Wow, Haley, I was really wrong about you. I thought you were smarter than that. And I thought Allison was too. But then she proved me wrong. She was so easily influenced by Sarah. She was weak. And she didn't understand. Not like I thought you would."

"So you killed her?" I asked him wearily. We were playing an odd game. He knew what I was doing and I knew what he was doing. But he didn't care. He knew he had me; he wanted to savor it. He needed to confess his deeds to someone and then kill them. He wanted someone to stroke his ego. We both paced the walls of the cave, going around and around and around.

"Yes, Haley, I killed her. I had to." He laughed. "You think I'd just let her go free? Break someone else's heart?"

"She didn't have to like you, Jonas. That's not fair. It doesn't work like that." The words came out of my mouth before I had the time to stop them. Jonas glared at me.

"Why not? I was good to her. Honest."

"You can't make someone love you." His glare only grew deeper, and for a moment I thought he was going to snap. "And what about Rebecca? Why did she have to die?"

"Because she was just like Allison. After all Noah did for her, she didn't care. She was fake too. And weak. She did anything Allison and Sarah told her to like a little puppy dog. Even after Allison was gone, Rebecca couldn't stop thinking about her. Thinking about what Allison would want her to do. People like that are followers, Haley. They're weak. And they'll end up hurting someone like Hannah hurt you."

"You're crazy!" I shouted. My phone started to ring in the corner of the cave.

"No, you're crazy. Hannah didn't love you. If she did, then she wouldn't have been so influenced by that other girl. She wouldn't have listened to her. Or left you."

"How do you even know about that?" I spat at him.

Jonas put his hand in his pocket and took out a notebook. The same one I'd thrown in the river that day with Rebecca. "Your father is a smart man, Haley. He took notes; he made sure he didn't make the wrong decision. I found this in the river where I killed Rebecca and I just knew I had to have it. It was his, wasn't it?" I nodded. Jonas smiled at the book. "That's why I killed her. Because I thought you were special and that she would hurt you. Just like Hannah did. She hurt Noah too. She was probably the one I enjoyed the most."

I shuddered. It was foreign to me how people could think such wicked thoughts. It was scary, but to stay alive I had to think like him. "And Sarah, although that one's clear."

He smiled scarily. "Now you're starting to understand. She should have been first, but the sneaky girl was never anywhere alone. I almost forgot about her for a while, until this afternoon. When she said all those things to you. And you slapped her." His smile grew. "You inspired me, Haley. And I thought you understood. She hurt you. So she had to go."

He suddenly kneeled down and gently laid the notebook on the floor of the cave. As he stood back up, he reached down and grabbed a rock off the ground. A very heavy, sharp rock. I was suddenly fixated on that rock. Really fixated. In the background I could hear my phone ringing, and suddenly I heard the faint wail of sirens. The cavalry was on the way, but they had better hurry up.

Jonas cursed under his breath. "You've asked so many questions, you've almost hit twenty," he joked cruelly. He stroked the rock with his finger. "You know how the game works. It's my turn to ask the questions. Why are you so afraid of me?"

"Because you killed three people! You ass!" I screamed.

Jonas looked disappointed. "If only your father could see you now, Haley. He saw something in you, and so did I. But I guess even the best of us make mistakes." Jonas lunged at me with the rock steady in his hand.

I screamed with everything I had. If I wasn't going to leave this cave alive, I at least wanted someone to know that this was where I had been. "Who hurt you so bad?" I yelled in a final attempt to slow him down.

"Who didn't?" he asked and suddenly lunged and grabbed my arm. I could hear the sirens growing louder. They couldn't be too far away now. I let out one final scream and looked into Jonas's eyes, which were wild with anger, and then the world went dark.

35

Ouch was the first thing I thought when I woke up again. Everything was so bright that I wanted to keep my eyes closed, but I was reluctant to return to the darkness.

When I finally committed to waking up, the walls of the tiny room I was in were impossibly white. Everything popped out at me like a bright sun in the middle of the night.

"She's up!" shouted a female voice beside me. I turned my head weakly to see who had interrupted my quiet moment. It was my mom. I think that was when I realized: I was alive! My memory wasn't very clear, and patches of it seemed to be blurry or gone like I was fast-forwarding through a movie. The only thoughts I could form clearly were Jonas's angry eyes and a stabbing pain.

"Mom?" I croaked. My throat was scratchier than I'd thought it would be.

She smiled at me and stroked my hair. "It's all right, baby. Everything's going to be all right. I've got you." Slow tears started to fall down her cheeks.

"What happened?" I asked her.

At first, she didn't respond. She was too busy hugging me, making sure she wasn't dreaming and I was really still there.

"That boy," she said after a while. "The one that came to our house." She started crying harder. "I didn't think you would make it. But you're a fighter, Haley. You always have been." I gave her the most convincing smile I could muster. A crushing feeling of guilt washed over me. How could I have put my mother through this? Why didn't I see it coming?

After a while, I convinced her that I needed some quiet time. I was finally told I had been out of it for a day. I had a bad concussion and two deep wounds in my thigh that had almost caused me to bleed out, but I would be okay.

My mother wasn't so convinced. She made the doctors and nurses run so many tests on me that I started to wish I had spent a few more days unconscious.

The next day, I was cleared to have other visitors, though I doubted anyone would come see me. Right as I started to drift off to sleep again, I heard a knock on the door. Probably just my mom making sure that I was still there and doing okay. "Come in," I called out.

To my surprise, it was Noah. He looked older than I had remembered. Bags hung under his eyes, and his hair was tousled and sticking up in every direction.

"Hey," he said.

"Hey, you," I said, smiling. I eased back into my bed. Noah wasn't here to hurt me, I was sure of that.

He pulled up a stool from the corner of the room, placed it next to my bed, and sat down. "How are you feeling?" he asked. I tried to shrug, but a burning pain from my leg where I had been stabbed shot up my back, causing me to wince instead. "Yeah, me too," said Noah. I laughed for the first time that day. We sat there for a minute not saying anything to each other, but that was okay. All I needed to know was that Noah was there.

After a while, I asked him, "Did you know?"

He shook his head. "Did you?"

"No," I told him. And I was afraid because it was the truth. Noah filled me in on what had happened before and after I'd ended up in the hospital. We went back to the beginning and worked our way up until we reached the cave.

Jonas had apparently heard about Dan Hansen at the beginning of the school year and had gotten infatuated with him, unbeknownst to us. After that, he was obsessed with finding the perfect people that he thought my father would have "wanted." We weren't really sure why he thought like this—or why my father did—but we knew that it had happened. My best guess was that he was just lonely and shy and tired of being ignored. After a while, he started to blame other people for the way he was.

Noah would often lend Jonas his computer because he never really used it, and he knew Jonas was into Photoshop and coding and stuff like that. What he hadn't known was that Jonas had created a Dan Hansen fan website and started to connect with some other very sick people. This only further convinced him that my dad was right, so he decided to carry out a mission, thinking it would please the congregation of followers.

Jonas started writing letters to Allison because he was convinced that she was like Dan Hansen's daughter—me—and he wanted to share this with her. When she rejected both him and his ideas, he decided to kill her. He used Photoshop to make all of the images he sent her and left a final one with her body.

What he didn't think would happen was Rebecca trying to help us solve the murder. Jonas and Rebecca weren't close, so he didn't know her very well. He thought she was just a ditzy but harmless girl, and that she was too dumb to realize how much Noah liked her.

When Jonas realized that she was actually quite smart and in love with Allison, he got angry because he knew that she and Noah would never be together. In a way, he thought that he was killing Rebecca for Noah, knowing he would end up brokenhearted after Rebecca ultimately rejected him.

He'd pocketed the photo from my room and arranged a meeting in the woods, telling Rebecca he had a personal question and not to tell anyone. That was when he killed her and took the journal. Once he had done the deed, he wiped the messages from both of their phones, but they were eventually recovered. He should have known that once you put something out there, it's never truly gone.

Then he found out that I was Dan Hansen's daughter and everything changed. Now I was the subject of his wicked obsession. He must have felt some remorse for the pain that he had caused me or he didn't want to look too suspicious, so he helped me with the investigation. He didn't want me to see the monster he really was. And as for Sarah, he despised her for the way she antagonized me. He saw her as the new Hannah and thought it was his duty to both me and my dad to get rid of her.

He tried attacking her, which was why he left Reynold's early. She got away that time, but when she went off on me after school, he decided to try again and succeeded. Then he hung out with Noah to give himself an alibi.

But then I let it slip to Cook and Green that Sarah had thought Noah was the killer. Cook found that the website originated from Noah's computer and confronted him about it, but he admitted that he hardly ever used his laptop and it was practically Jonas's. His story checked out once they checked the IP address of the website. It was from Jonas's home Wi-Fi. After that, everything fell into place. When I didn't respond to Noah's calls, they figured that Jonas had probably gone after me somewhere in the woods, just like he had with Sarah and Rebecca, but they didn't know where, so they sent out a search team. When I texted Noah that I was in the cave, they made a mad rush and found me seconds after Jonas had rocked me. This morning, they'd tested his DNA against evidence found at the scene and discovered that it was a match. With the forensic evidence and me as a witness, his fate was pretty much sealed. He was going to rot in prison. I secretly hoped they would somehow manage to put him in a cell with my dad so they could grow old together in a small, quiet room with no windows.

I sighed. "So it's over?"

"It's over," Noah confirmed. We were both silent. What was going to happen to us now?

"It'll never be over," I said as my voice cracked.

Noah squeezed my shoulder harder. "You can't say that."

I looked at his face. It was a cross between upset and concerned.

"Why not? It's true. Wherever I go, whatever I do, bad people are going to follow me."

"That's just because bad people are everywhere, Haley. There's nothing we can do about it—except not be bad."

But I really couldn't get away. That was simply not a luxury I had. How many Jonases were out there?

36

June 13, 2019

After making up at school, Hannah and I decided to head back to my house again after picking up food at a local cafe. It was far too hot outside, causing us to retreat from our usual spot on the hammock to the safe, cool cavity of my room. We sat on my bed with our legs criss-cross applesauce, chewing away at our food.

Even though everything was supposed to be back to normal, there was an unspoken tension in the air. I could tell that Hannah felt it too.

"Okay, what's wrong?" I asked between bites of sandwich. "Is there something you're not telling me?"

"Nothing," Hannah said, shaking her head while gnawing on salad. She didn't look too sure.

"You're lying." I knew her better than anyone. Even if she denied it, I knew that something was up.

"Jesus Christ, Haley, can you just let it drop?" she advised me in an annoyed tone, but she continued eating.

I scrunched my eyebrows. "No! I need to know that everything's okay between us. You seem annoyed."

"Well, obviously because you keep pestering me. Can't you let anything go?" Hannah glared back at me.

My head pounded angrily. No, I couldn't let anything go, not if she was keeping something from me. Plus I had seen her talking to Claire earlier. *What if us making up was an elaborate ruse? What if they're plotting against me in some way? What if, what if, what if, what if?* "But you—" I started.

"Stop!" She threw her plastic cutlery onto my bed. "This is why I'm the only one who puts up with you. Your paranoia is too much! It's driving me insane! You're so freakin' insecure. It's exhausting."

I clutched my head in my hands, trying to soothe the throbbing. "Oh, and I bet Claire is super secure?" The pain was becoming too much. I could hardly think straight, much less control the words coming out of my mouth.

Hannah laughed like I had just told the funniest joke in the world that I somehow wasn't in on. "Yeah, she is. At least more than you. I can't put up with this anymore. We're done." She grabbed her bag bitterly and moved towards the door. "I'm leaving, and I won't be back."

Just as she was about to grab the doorknob, the pain became so much that it was blinding. All my senses were heightened to the max, but I could hardly process anything. "No!" I shouted. I needed her to come back so I could explain myself. If only …

"What, are you going to stop me?" Hannah chuckled. The sound amplified in my ears, sending ripples throughout my head. It was unbearable. Just for a moment, I needed it to stop … I needed Hannah to stop.

Stop …

Stop …

Stop …

"Stop!" I screamed with all my might. I grasped the knife Hannah had been using to eat her salad. Without thinking, I sliced into her abdomen.

Hannah opened her mouth in a shocked "o," silent for the first time in her life. She clutched her stomach where the knife had gone in, stumbling backward. A thick, heavy circle of blood started to expand around the wound. She looked down, and finally, she collapsed like a rag doll on the floor of the room.

I exhaled.

Finally, it was quiet. I'd made the noise stop, but I was exhausted. And the headache hadn't gone away. A final surge of pain shot up to my skull, and it was too much. There was nothing else to do but ... nothing at all. Shrieking in pain, I allowed myself to fall to the floor next to Hannah.

The next thing I knew, I was lying in bed and Hannah was gone. I rubbed my head. I couldn't quite remember, but I could have sworn that I had told Hannah I needed a nap and sent her home. Maybe it was a dream, but either way, she was gone.

There was nothing to do but sit in my room and do some homework.

Made in the USA
Middletown, DE
05 September 2022

73228135R00120